FIVE GO OFF
TO CAMP

ENID BLYTON

**Hodder
Children's
Books**

A division of Hachette Children's Books

Copyright © Enid Blyton Ltd.
Enid Blyton's signature mark and the Famous Five
are trademarks of Enid Blyton Limited.

First published in Great Britain in 1947
by Hodder and Stoughton

This edition 2001

The right of Enid Blyton to be identified as the Author of
the Work has been asserted by her in accordance with the
Copyright, Designs and Patents Act 1988.

10

British Library C.I.P.

Blyton, Enid
    Five Go Off to Camp –
    (Blyton, Enid. Famous Five).
    I. Title
    823'.9'1J   PZ7.B629

ISBN-10: 0 340 79621 9
ISBN-13: 978 0340 79621 4

Typeset by Hewer Text Ltd, Edinburgh
Printed and bound in Great Britain by
Clays Ltd, St Ives plc

The paper and board used in this paperback by Hodder
Children's Books are natural recyclable products made from
wood grown in sustainable forests. The manufacturing processes
conform to the environmental regulations of the country of origin.

Hodder Children's Books
a division of Hachette Children's Books
338 Euston Road
London NW1 3BH

Contents

[1]

Holiday Time

'Two jolly fine tents, four groundsheets, four sleeping-bags – I say, what about Timmy? Isn't he going to have a sleeping-bag too?' said Dick, with a grin.

The other three children laughed, and Timmy, the dog, thumped his tail hard on the ground.

'Look at him,' said George. 'He's laughing, too! He's got his mouth stretched wide open.'

They all looked at Timmy. He really did look as if a wide grin stretched his hairy mouth from side to side.

'He's a darling,' said Anne, hugging him. 'Best dog in the world, aren't you, Timmy?'

'Woof!' said Timmy, agreeing. He gave Anne a wet lick on her nose.

The four children, Julian, tall and strong for

his age, Dick, George and Anne were busy planning a camping holiday. George was a girl, not a boy, but she would never answer to her real name, Georgina. With her freckled face and short, curly hair she really did look more like a boy than a girl.

'It's absolutely wizard, being allowed to go on a camping holiday all by ourselves,' said Dick. 'I never thought our parents would allow it, after the terrific adventure we had last summer, when we went off in caravans.'

'Well – we shan't be *quite* all by ourselves,' said Anne. 'Don't forget we've got Mr Luffy to keep an eye on us. He'll be camping quite near.

'Pooh! Old Luffy!' said Dick, with a laugh. 'He won't know if we're there or not. So long as he can study his precious moorland insects, he won't bother about us.'

'Well, if it hadn't been that he was going to camp, too, we wouldn't have been allowed to go,' said Anne. 'I heard Daddy say so.'

Mr Luffy was a master at the boys' school, an elderly, dreamy fellow with a passion for studying all kinds of insect-life. Anne avoided him when he carried about boxes of insect specimens, because sometimes they escaped and came crawling out. The boys liked him and thought him fun, but the idea of Mr Luffy keeping an eye on them struck them as very comical.

'It's more likely we'll have to keep an eye on *him*,' said Julian. 'He's the sort of chap whose tent will always be falling down on top of him, or he'll run out of water, or sit down on his bag of eggs. Old Luffy seems to live in the world of insects, not in our world!'

'Well, he can go and live in the world of insects if he likes, so long as he doesn't interfere with *us*,' said George, who hated interfering people. 'This sounds as if it will be a super holiday – living in tents on the high moors, away from everybody, doing exactly what we like, when we like and how we like.'

'Woof!' said Timmy, thumping his tail again.

'That means he's going to do as *he* likes, too,' said Anne. 'You're going to chase hundreds of rabbits, aren't you, Timmy, and bark madly at anyone who dares to come within two miles of us!'

'Now be quiet a minute, Anne!' said Dick, picking up his list again. 'We really must check down our list and find out if we've got every single thing we want. Where did I get to – oh, four sleeping-bags.'

'Yes, and you wanted to know if Timmy was to have one,' said Anne, with a giggle.

'Of course he won't,' said George. 'He'll sleep where he always does – won't you, Timmy? On my feet.'

'Couldn't we get him just a *small* sleeping-bag?' asked Anne. 'He'd look sweet with his head poking out of the top.'

'Timmy hates looking sweet,' said George. 'Go on, Dick. I'll tie my hanky round Anne's mouth if she interrupts again.'

Dick went on down his list. It was a very interesting one. Things like cooking-stoves, canvas buckets, enamel plates and drinking-cups were on it and each item seemed to need a lot of discussion. The four children enjoyed themselves very much.

'You know, it's almost as much fun planning a holiday like this as having it,' said Dick. 'Well – I shouldn't think we've forgotten a thing, have we?'

'No. We've probably thought of too much!' said Julian. 'Well, old Luffy says he'll take all our things on the trailer behind his car, so we'll be all right. I shouldn't like to carry them ourselves!'

'Oh, I wish next week would come!' said Anne. 'Why is it that the time seems so long when you're waiting for something nice to happen, and so short when something nice *is* happening?'

'Yes, it seems the wrong way round, doesn't it?' said Dick, with a grin. 'Anyone got the map? I'd like to take another squint at the spot where we're going.'

Julian produced a map from his pocket. He opened it and the four children sprawled round it. The map showed a vast and lonely stretch of moorland, with very few houses indeed.

'Just a few small farms, that's all,' said Julian pointing to one or two. 'They can't get much of a living out of such poor land, though. See, that's about the place where we're going – just there – and on the opposite slope is a small farm where we shall get milk, eggs and butter when we need them. Luffy's been there before. He says it's a rather small farm, but jolly useful to campers.'

'These moors are awfully high, aren't they?' said George. 'I guess they'll be freezing cold in the winter.'

'They are,' said Julian. 'And they may be jolly windy and cold in the summer, too, so Luffy says we'd better take sweaters and things. He says in the winter they are covered with snow for months. The sheep have to be dug out when they get lost.'

Dick's finger followed a small winding road that made its way over the wild stretch of moorland. 'That's the road we go,' he said. 'And I suppose we strike off here, look, where a cart-track is shown. That would go to the farm. We shall have to carry our stuff from wherever Luffy parks his car, and take it to our camping-place.'

'Not too near Luffy, I hope,' said George.

'Oh, no. He's agreed to keep an eye on us, but he'll forget all about us once he's settled down in his own tent,' said Julian. 'He will, really. Two chaps I know once went out in his car with him for a day's run, and he came back without them in the evening. He'd forgotten he had them with him, and had left them wandering somewhere miles and miles away.'

'Good old Luffy,' said Dick. 'That's the sort of fellow we want! He won't come springing up to ask if we've cleaned our teeth or if we've got our warm jerseys on!'

The others laughed, and Timmy stretched his doggy mouth into a grin again. His tongue hung out happily. It was good to have all four of his friends with him again, and to hear them planning a holiday. Timmy went to school with George and Anne in term time, and he missed the two boys very much. But he belonged to

George, and would not dream of leaving her. It was a good thing that George's school allowed pets, or George would certainly not have gone!

Julian folded up the map again. 'I hope all the things we've ordered will come in good time,' he said. 'We've got about six days to wait. I'd better keep on reminding Luffy that we're going with him, or he's quite likely to start without us!'

It was difficult to have to wait so long now that everything was planned. Parcels came from various stores and were eagerly opened. The sleeping-bags were fine.

'Super!' said Anne.

'Smashing!' said George, crawling into hers. 'Look! I can lace it up at the neck – and it's got a hood thing to come right over my head. Golly, it's warm! I shan't mind the coldest night if I'm sleeping in this. I vote we sleep in them tonight.'

'What? In our bedrooms?' said Anne.

'Yes. Why not? Just to get used to them,' said George, who felt that a sleeping-bag was a hundred times better than an ordinary bed.

So that night all four slept on the floor of their bedrooms in their sleeping-bags, and voted them very comfortable and as warm as toast.

'The only thing is, Timmy kept wanting to come right inside mine,' said George, 'and honestly there isn't enough room. Besides, he'd be cooked.'

'Well, he seemed to spend half the night on my tummy,' grumbled Julian. 'I shall jolly well keep the bedroom door shut if Timmy's going to spend the night flopping on everyone's bag in turn.'

'I don't mind the flopping, so much as the frightful habit he's got of turning himself round and round and round before he flops down,' complained Dick. 'He did that on me last night. Silly habit of his.'

'He can't help it,' said George at once. 'It's a habit that wild dogs had centuries and centuries ago – they slept in reeds and rushes, and they got into the way of turning themselves round and round in them, to trample them down and make themselves a good sleeping-place. And our dogs go on turning themselves round now, before they go to sleep, even though there aren't any rushes to trample down.'

'Well! I wish Timmy would forget his doggy ancestors were wild dogs with rushy beds, and just remember he's a nice tame dog with a basket of his own,' said Dick. 'You should see my tummy today! It's all printed over with his foot-marks.'

'Fibber!' said Anne. 'You do exaggerate, Dick. Oh, I do wish Tuesday would come. I'm tired of waiting.'

'It'll come all right,' said Julian. And so it did, of course. It dawned bright and sunny, with a sky that was a deep blue, flecked with tiny white clouds.

'Good-weather clouds,' said Julian, pleased. 'Now let's hope old Luffy has remembered it's today we're starting off. He's due here at ten o'clock. We're taking sandwiches for the whole party. Mother thought we'd better, in case Luffy forgot his. If he's remembered them it won't matter, because we're sure to be able to eat them ourselves. And there's always Timmy to finish things up!'

Timmy was as excited as the four children. He always knew when something nice was going to happen. His tail was on the wag the whole time, his tongue hung out, and he panted as if he had been running a race. He kept getting under everyone's feet, but nobody minded.

Mr Luffy arrived half an hour late, just when everyone was beginning to feel he had forgotten to come. He was at the wheel of his big old car, beaming. All the children knew him quite well, because he lived not far away and often came to play bridge with their father and mother.

'Hallo, hallo!' he cried. 'All ready, I see! Good for you! Pile the things on the trailer, will you? Mine are there too but there's plenty of room. I've got sandwiches for everyone, by the way. My wife said I'd better bring plenty.'

'We'll have a fine feast today then,' said Dick, helping Julian to carry out the folded-up tents and sleeping-bags, while the girls

followed with the smaller things. Soon everything was on the trailer and Julian made them
safe with ropes.

They said goodbye to the watching grown-
ups and climbed excitedly into the car. Mr Luffy
started up his engine and put the lever into first
gear with a frightful noise.

'Goodbye!' called all the grown-ups, and
Julian's mother added a last word. 'DON'T
get into any awful adventure this time!'

'Of course they won't!' called back Mr Luffy
cheerfully. 'I'll see to that. There are no adventures to be found on a wild and deserted moor.
Goodbye!'

Off they went, waving madly, and shouting
goodbye all the way down the road. 'Goodbye!
Goodbyeeeeee! Hurrah, we're off at last!'

The car raced down the road, the trailer
bumping madly after it. The holiday had be-
gun!

[2]

Up on the moors

Mr Luffy was not a good driver. He went too fast, especially round the corners, and many times Julian looked behind at the trailer in alarm, afraid that everything would suddenly leap off it at some sharp bend.

He saw the bundle of sleeping-bags jump high into the air, but fortunately they remained on the trailer. He touched Mr Luffy on the shoulder.

'Sir! Could you go a bit slower, please! The trailer will be empty by the time we arrive, if the luggage leaps about on it much more.'

'My word! I forgot we had a trailer,' said Mr Luffy, slowing down at once. 'Remind me if I go over thirty-five miles an hour, will you? Last time I took the trailer with me, I arrived with only half the goods on it. I don't want that to happen again.'

Julian certainly hoped it wouldn't. He kept a sharp eye on the speedometer, and when it veered towards forty he tapped Mr Luffy on the arm.

Mr Luffy looked supremely happy. He didn't like term time, but he loved holidays. Term time interfered with the study of his beloved insect-world. Now he was off with four nice children he liked, for a holiday on a moorland he knew was alive with bees, beetles, butterflies and every other kind of insect he wanted. He looked forward to teaching the four children quite a lot. They would have been horrified if they guessed this, but they didn't.

He was an odd-looking fellow. He had very untidy, shaggy eyebrows over kind and gentle brown eyes that always reminded Dick of a monkey's. He had a rather large nose, which looked fiercer than it was because, unexpectedly, it had quite a forest of hairs growing out of the nostrils. He had an untidy moustache, and a round chin with a surprising dimple in the middle of it.

His ears always fascinated Anne. They were large and turned rather forward, and Mr Luffy could waggle the right one if he wanted to. To his great sorrow he had never been able to waggle the left one. His hair was thick and untidy, and his clothes always looked loose, comfortable and rather too big for him.

The children liked him. They couldn't help it. He was so odd and gentle and untidy and forgetful – and yet sometimes unexpectedly fierce. Julian had often told them the story of Tom Killin the bully.

Mr Luffy had once found Tom bullying a small new boy in the cloakroom, dragging him round and round it by his belt. With a roar like an angry bull, Mr Luffy had pounced on the big bully, got him by the belt, lifted him up and stuck him firmly on a peg in the cloakroom.

'There you stay till you get someone to lift you down!' Mr Luffy had thundered. '*I* can get hold of a belt too, as you can see!'

And then he had stalked out of the cloakroom with the small, terrified boy beside him, leaving the bully hung up high on the peg, quite unable to free himself. And there he had to stay, because not one of the boys who came pouring in from a game of football would lift him down.

'And, if the peg hadn't given way under his weight, he'd be stuck up there still,' Julian had said with a grin. 'Good old Luffy! You'd never think he could be fierce like that, would you?'

Anne loved that story. Mr Luffy became quite a hero to her after that. She was pleased to sit next to him in the car, and chatter about all kinds of things. The other three were squashed at the back with Timmy on their feet. George firmly prevented him from climbing up on her knee because it was so hot. So he contented himself with trying to stand up with his paws on the window-ledge and his nose over the side.

They stopped about half past twelve for lunch. Mr Luffy had indeed provided sandwiches for everyone. And remarkably fine ones they were too, made the evening before by Mrs Luffy.

'Cucumber, dipped in vinegar! Ham and lettuce! Egg! Sardine! Oooh, Mr Luffy, your sandwiches are much nicer than ours,' said Anne, beginning on two together, one cucumber and the other ham and lettuce.

They were all very hungry. Timmy had a bit from everyone, usually the last bite, and watched each sandwich eagerly till his turn came. Mr Luffy didn't seem to understand that Timmy had to have the last bite of any sandwich, so Timmy simply took it out of his hand, much to his surprise.

'A clever dog,' he said, and patted him. 'Knows what he wants and takes it. Very clever.'

That pleased George, of course. She thought that Timmy was the cleverest dog in the world, and indeed it did seem like it at times. He understood every word she said to him, every pat, every stroke, every gesture. He would be much, much better at keeping an eye on the four children and guarding them than forgetful Mr Luffy.

They drank ginger-beer and then ate some ripe plums. Timmy wouldn't have any plums, but he licked up some spilt ginger-beer. Then he snuffed up a few odd crumbs and went to drink at a little stream nearby.

The party set off again in the car. Anne fell asleep. Dick gave an enormous yawn and fell asleep too. George wasn't sleepy, nor was Timmy, but Julian was. He didn't dare to take his eye off the speedometer, though, because Mr Luffy seemed to be very much inclined to speed along too fast again, after his good lunch.

'We won't stop for tea till we get there,' said Mr Luffy suddenly, and Dick woke up with a jump at the sound of his booming voice. 'We should be there about half past five. Look, you can see the moorland in the distance now – all ablaze with heather!'

Everybody looked ahead, except Anne, who was still fast asleep. Rising up to the left for miles upon miles was the heather-covered moorland, a lovely sight to see. It looked wild and lonely and beautiful, blazing with heather, and shading off into a purple-blue in the distance.

'We take this road to the left, and then we're on the moors,' said Mr Luffy, swinging violently to the left, and making the luggage in the trailer jump high again. 'Here we go.'

The car climbed the high moorland road steadily. It passed one or two small houses, and in the distance the children could see little farms in clearings. Sheep dotted the moorland, and some of them stood staring at the car as it drove by.

'We've got about twenty miles to go, I should think,' said Mr Luffy, jamming on his brakes suddenly to avoid two large sheep in the middle of the road. 'I wish these creatures wouldn't choose the centre of the road to gossip in. Hi, get on there! Let me pass!'

Timmy yelped and tried to get out of the car. The sheep hurriedly decided to move, and the car went on. Anne was thoroughly awake by now, having been almost jerked out of her seat by the sudden stop.

'What a shame to wake you!' said Mr Luffy, gazing down at her kindly, and almost running into a ditch by the side of the road. 'We're nearly there, Anne.'

They climbed steadily, and the wind grew a little cold. All around the children the moors stretched for mile upon mile, never-ending. Little streams sometimes splashed right down to the roadway, and ran beside it.

'We can drink the water in these streams,' said Mr Luffy. 'Crystal clear, and cold as ice! There's one quite near where we're going to camp.'

That was good news. Julian thought of the big canvas buckets they had brought. He didn't particularly want to carry those for miles. If there was a stream near their camping-place it would be easy to get the buckets filled with washing-water.

The road forked into two. To the right was a good road, leading on and on. To the left it became not much more than a cart-track. 'That's the one we take,' said Mr Luffy, and the car jerked and jolted over it. He was forced to go slowly, and the children had time to see every little thing they passed.

'I shall leave the car here,' said Mr Luffy, bringing it to a standstill beside a great rock that stood up bare and grey out of the moor. 'It will be sheltered from the worst winds and rain. I thought we'd camp over yonder.'

There was a little slope just there, backed by some enormous gorse bushes. Thick heather grew everywhere. Julian nodded. It was a good place for camping. Those thick gorse bushes would provide fine shelter from the winds.

'Right, sir,' he said. 'Shall we have tea first, or unpack now?'

'Tea first,' said Mr Luffy. 'I've brought a very good little stove for boiling and cooking things. Better than a wood fire. That makes kettles and saucepans so black.'

'We've got a stove, too,' said Anne. She scrambled out of the car and looked all round. 'It's lovely here – all heather and wind and sun!

Is that the farm over there – the one we shall go to for eggs and things?'

She pointed to a tiny farmhouse on the hill opposite. It stood in a small clearing. In a field behind it were three or four cows and a horse. A small orchard stood at the side, and a vegetable garden lay in front. It seemed odd to see such a trim little place in the midst of the moorland.

'That's Olly's Farm,' said Mr Luffy. 'It's changed hands, I believe, since I was here three years ago. I hope the new people are nice. Now – did we leave something to eat for our tea?'

They had, because Anne had wisely put away a good many sandwiches and bits of cake for tea-time. They sat in the heather, with bees humming all round them, and munched solidly for fifteen minutes. Timmy waited patiently for his bits, watching the bees that hummed round him. There were thousands of them.

'And now I suppose we'd better put up our tents,' said Julian. 'Come on, Dick – let's un-pack the trailer. Mr Luffy, we don't intend to camp on top of you, sir, because you won't want four noisy children too near. Where would you like your tent put?'

Mr Luffy was about to say that he would like to have the four children and Timmy quite close, when it suddenly occurred to him that perhaps they might not want him too near. They might want to make a noise, or play silly games, and if he were near it would stop them enjoying themselves in their own way.

So he made up his mind not to be too close. 'I'll pitch my tent down there, where that old gorse bush is,' he said. 'And if you'd like to put yours up here, where there's a half-circle of gorse bushes keeping off the wind, you'd be well sheltered. And we shan't interfere with one another at all.'

'Right, sir,' said Julian, and he and Dick began to tackle the tents. It was fun. Timmy got under everyone's feet as usual, and ran off with an important rope, but nobody minded.

By the time that dusk came creeping up the heather-covered moorland, all three tents were up, the groundsheets were put down, and the

sleeping-bags unrolled on them, two in each of
the children's tents, and one in Mr Luffy's.

'I'm going to turn in,' said Mr Luffy. 'My
eyes are almost shut. Good-night all of you.
Sleep well!'

He disappeared into the dusk. Anne yawned
widely, and that set the others off too. 'Come
on – let's turn in, too,' said Julian. 'We'll have a
bar of chocolate each, and a few biscuits. We
can eat those in our sleeping-bags. Good-night,
girls. Won't it be grand to wake up tomorrow
morning?'

He and Dick disappeared into their tent. The
girls crawled into theirs with Timmy. They
undressed, and got into their warm, soft sleeping-bags.

'This is super!' said George, pushing Timmy
to one side. 'I never felt so cosy in my life.
Don't do that, Timmy. Don't you know the
difference between my feet and my middle?
That's better.'

'Good-night,' said Anne, sleepily. 'Look,
George, you can see the stars shining through

the opening of the tent. Don't they look enormous?'

But George didn't care whether they were enormous or not. She was fast asleep, tired out with the day's run. Timmy cocked one ear when he heard Anne's voice, and gave a little grunt. That was his way of saying good-night. Then he put his head down and slept.

'Our first night of camping,' thought Anne, happily. 'I shan't go to sleep. I shall lie awake and look at the stars and smell that heathery smell.'

But she didn't. In half a second she was sound asleep, too!

[3]

Anne's volcano

Julian awoke first in the morning. He heard a strange and lonely sound floating overhead. 'Coor-lie! Coor-lie!'

He sat up and wondered where he was and who was calling. Of course! He was in his tent with Dick – they were camping on the moors. And that wild cry overhead came from a curlew, the bird of the moorlands.

He yawned and lay down again. It was early in the morning. The sun put its warm fingers in at his tent opening, and he felt the warmth on his sleeping-bag. He felt lazy and snug and contented. He also felt hungry, which was a nuisance. He glanced at his watch.

Half past six. He really was too warm and comfortable to get up yet. He put out his hand to see if there was any chocolate left from the night before, and found a little piece. He put it into his mouth and lay there contentedly, listening to more curlews, and watching the sun climb a little higher.

He fell asleep again, and was awakened by Timmy busily licking his face. He sat up with a start. The girls were peering in at his tent, grinning. They were fully dressed already.

'Wake up, lazy!' said Anne. 'We sent Timmy in to get you up. It's half past seven. We've been up for ages.'

'It's a simply heavenly morning,' said George. 'Going to be a frightfully hot day. Do get up. We're going to find the stream and wash in it. It seems silly to lug heavy buckets of water to and fro for washing, if the stream's nearby.'

Dick awoke too. He and Julian decided to go and take a bathe in the stream. They wandered out into the sunny morning, feeling very happy and very hungry. The girls were just coming back from the stream.

'It's over there,' said Anne, pointing. 'Tim-my, go with them and show them. It's a lovely little brown stream, awfully cold, and it's got ferns along its banks. We've left the bucket there. Bring it back full, will you?'

'What do you want us to do that for, if you've already washed?' asked Dick.

'We want water for washing-up the dishes,' said Anne. 'I suddenly remembered we'd need water for that. I say, do you think we ought to wake up Mr Luffy? There's no sign of him yet.'

'No, let him sleep,' said Julian. 'He's probably tired out with driving the car so slowly! We can easily save him some breakfast. What are we going to have?'

'We've unpacked some bacon rashers and tomatoes,' said Anne, who loved cooking. 'How do you light the stove, Julian?'

'George knows,' said Julian. 'I say, did we pack a frying-pan?'

'Yes. I packed it myself,' said Anne. 'Do go and bathe if you're going to. Breakfast will be ready before you are!'

Timmy gravely trotted off with the boys and showed them the stream. Julian and Dick at once lay down in the clear brown bed, and kicked wildly. Timmy leapt in too, and there were yells and shrieks.

'Well – I should think we've woken up old Luffy now!' said Dick, rubbing himself down with a rough towel. 'How lovely and cold that was. The trouble is it's made me feel twice as hungry!'

'Doesn't that frying bacon smell good?' said Julian, sniffing the air. They walked back to the girls. There was still no sign of Mr Luffy. He must indeed sleep very soundly!

They sat down in the heather and began their breakfast. Anne had fried big rounds of bread in the fat, and the boys told her she was the best cook in the world. She was very pleased.

'I shall look after the food side for you,' she said. 'But George must help with the preparing of the meals and washing-up. See, George?'

George didn't see. She hated doing all the things that Anne loved to do, such as making beds and washing-up. She looked sulky.

'Look at old George! Why bother about the

washing-up when there's Timmy only too pleased to use his tongue to wash every plate?' said Dick.

Everyone laughed, even George. 'All right,' she said, 'I'll help of course. Only let's use as few plates as possible, then there won't be much washing-up. Is there any more fried bread, Anne?'

'No. But there are some biscuits in that tin,' said Anne. 'I say, boys, who's going to go to the farm each day for milk and things? I expect they can let us have bread, too, and fruit.'

'Oh, one or other of us will go,' said Dick. 'Anne, hadn't you better fry something for old Luffy now? I'll go and wake him. Half the day will be gone if he doesn't get up now.'

'I'll go and make a noise like an earwig outside his tent,' said Julian, getting up. 'He might not wake with all our yells and shouts, but he'd certainly wake at the call of a friendly earwig!'

He went down to the tent. He cleared his throat and called politely: 'Are you awake yet, sir?'

There was no answer. Julian called again. Then, puzzled, he went to the tent opening. The flap was closed. He pulled it aside and looked in.

The tent was empty! There was nobody there at all.

'What's up, Ju?' called Dick.

'He's not here,' said Julian. 'Where can he be?'

There was silence. For a panic-stricken moment Anne thought one of their strange adventures was beginning. Then Dick called out again: 'Is his bug-tin gone? You know, the tin box with straps that he takes with him when he goes insect-hunting? And what about his clothes?'

Julian inspected the inside of the tent again. 'OK!' he called, much to everyone's relief. 'His clothes are gone, and so has his bug-tin. He must have slipped out early before we were awake. I bet he's forgotten all about us and breakfast and everything!'

'That would be just like him,' said Dick. 'Well, we're not his keepers. He can do as he likes! If he doesn't want breakfast, he needn't have any. He'll come back when he's finished his hunting, I suppose.'

'Anne! Can you get on with the doings if Dick and I go to the farmhouse and see what food they've got?' asked Julian. 'The time's getting on, and if we're going for a walk or anything today, we don't want to start too late.'

'Right,' said Anne. 'You go too, George. I can manage everything nicely, now that the boys have brought me a bucketful of water. Take Timmy. He wants a walk.'

George was only too pleased to get out of the washing-up. She and the boys, with Timmy trotting in front, set off to the farmhouse. Anne got on with her jobs, humming softly to herself in the sunshine. She soon finished them, and then looked to see if the others were coming back. There was no sign of them, or of Mr Luffy either.

'I'll go for a walk on my own,' thought Anne. 'I'll follow that little stream uphill and see where it begins. That would be fun. I can't possibly lose my way if I keep by the water.'

She set off in the sunshine and came to the little brown stream that gurgled down the hill. She scrambled through the heather beside it, following its course uphill. She liked all the little green ferns and the cushions of velvety moss that edged it. She tasted the water – it was cold and sweet and clean.

Feeling very happy all by herself, Anne walked on and on. She came at last to a big mound of a hill-top. The little stream began there, half-way up the mound. It came gurgling out of the heathery hillside, edged with moss, and made its chattering way far down the hill.

'So that's where you begin, is it?' said Anne. She flung herself down on the heather, hot with her climb. It was nice there, with the sun on her face, and the sound of the trickling water nearby.

She lay listening to the humming bees and the water. And then she heard another sound. She took no notice of it at all at first.

Then she sat up, frightened. 'The noise is underground! Deep, deep underground! It rumbles and roars. Oh, what is going to happen? Is there going to be an earthquake?'

The rumbling seemed to come nearer and nearer. Anne didn't even dare to get up and run. She sat there and trembled.

Then there came an unearthly shriek, and not far off a most astonishing thing happened. A great cloud of white smoke came right out of the ground and hung in the air before the wind blew it away. Anne was simply horrified. It was so sudden, so very unexpected on this quiet hillside. The rumbling noise went on for a while and then gradually faded away.

Anne leapt to her feet in a panic. She fled down the hill, screaming loudly: 'It's a volcano! Help! Help! I've been sitting on a volcano. It's going to burst, it's sending out smoke. Help, help, it's a VOLCANO!'

She tore down the hillside, caught her foot on a tuft of heather and went rolling over and over, sobbing. She came to rest at last, and then heard an anxious voice calling:

'Who's that? What's the matter?'

It was Mr Luffy's voice. Anne screamed to him in relief. 'Mr Luffy! Come and save me! There's a volcano here!'

There was such terror in her voice that Mr Luffy came racing to her at once. He sat down beside the trembling girl and put his arm round her. 'Whatever's the matter?' he said. 'What's frightened you?'

Anne told him again. 'Up there – do you see? That's a volcano, Mr Luffy. It trembled and rumbled and then it shot up clouds of smoke. Oh quick, before it sends out red hot cinders!'

'Now, now!' said Mr Luffy, and to Anne's surprise and relief he actually laughed. 'Do you mean to tell me you don't know what that was?'

'No, I don't,' said Anne.

'Well,' said Mr Luffy, 'under this big moor run two or three long tunnels to take trains from one valley to another. Didn't you know? They make the rumbling noise you heard, and the sudden smoke you saw was the smoke sent up by a train below. There are big vent-holes here and there in the moor for the smoke to escape from.'

'Oh, good gracious me!' said Anne, going rather red. 'I didn't even *know* there were trains under here. What an extraordinary thing! I really did think I was sitting on a volcano, Mr Luffy. You won't tell the others will you? They would laugh at me dreadfully.'

'I won't say a word,' said Mr Luffy. 'And now I think we'll go back. Have you had breakfast? I'm terribly hungry. I went out early after a rather rare butterfly I saw flying by my tent.'

'We've had breakfast *ages* ago,' said Anne. 'But if you'd like to come back with me now I'll cook you some bacon, Mr Luffy. And some tomatoes and fried bread.'

'Aha! It sounds good,' said Mr Luffy. 'Now – not a word about volcanoes. That's our secret.'

And off they went to the tents, where the others were wondering what in the world had become of Anne. Little did they know she had been 'sitting on a volcano'!

[4]

Spook-trains

The boys and George were full of talk about the farm. 'It's a nice little place,' said Julian, sitting down while Anne began to cook breakfast for Mr Luffy. 'Pretty farmhouse, nice little dairy, well-kept sheds. And even a grand piano in the drawing-room.'

'Gracious! You wouldn't think they'd make enough money to buy a thing like that, would you?' said Anne, turning over the bacon in the pan.

'The farmer's got a fine car,' went on Julian. 'Brand new. Must have cost him a pretty penny. His boy showed it to us. And he showed us some jolly good new farm machinery too.'

'Very interesting,' said Mr Luffy. 'I wonder how they make their money, farming that bit of land? The last people were hard-working folk, but they certainly couldn't have afforded a new car or a grand piano.'

'And you should have seen the lorries they've got!' said Dick. 'Beauties! Old army ones, I should think. The boy said his father's going to use them for carting things from the farm to the market.'

'What things?' said Mr Luffy, looking across at the little farmhouse. 'I shouldn't have thought they needed an army of lorries for that! An old farm wagon would carry all *their* produce.'

'Well, that's what he told us,' said Dick. 'Everything certainly looked very prosperous, I must say. He must be a jolly good farmer.'

'We got eggs and butter and fruit, and even some bacon,' said George. 'The boy's mother didn't seem worried about how much we had, and she hardly charged us anything. We didn't see the farmer.'

Mr Luffy was now eating his breakfast. He was certainly very hungry. He brushed away the flies that hung round his head, and when one settled on his right ear he waggled it violently. The fly flew off in surprise.

'Oh, do that again!' begged Anne. 'How do you do it? Do you think if I practised hard for weeks I could make my ear move?'

'No, I don't think so,' said Mr Luffy, finishing his breakfast. 'Well, I've got some writing to do now. What are you going to do? Go for a walk?'

'We might as well take a picnic lunch and go off somewhere,' said Julian. 'How about it?'

'Yes,' said Dick. 'Can you pack us dinner and tea, Anne? We'll help. What about hard-boiled eggs?'

It wasn't long before they had a picnic meal packed in greaseproof paper.

'You won't get lost, will you?' said Mr Luffy.

'Oh no, sir,' said Julian, with a laugh. 'I've got a compass, anyway, and a jolly good bump of locality, too. I usually know the way to go. We'll see you this evening, when we get back.'

'*You* won't get lost, Mr Luffy, will you?' asked Anne, looking worried.

'Don't be cheeky, Anne,' said Dick, rather horrified at Anne's question. But she really meant it. Mr Luffy was so absent-minded that she could quite well picture him wandering off and not being able to find his way back.

He smiled at her. 'No,' he said. 'I know my way about here all right – I know every stream and path and er – volcano!'

Anne giggled. The others stared at Mr Luffy, wondering what in the world he meant, but neither he nor Anne told them. They said goodbye and set off.

'It's heavenly walking today,' said Anne. 'Shall we follow a path if we find one or not?'

'Might as well,' said Julian. 'It'll be a bit tiring scrambling through heather all the day.'

So when they did unexpectedly come across a path they followed it. 'It's just a shepherd's path, I expect,' said Dick. 'I bet it's a lonely job, looking after sheep up on these desolate heathery hills.'

They went on for some way, enjoying the stretches of bright heather, the lizards that darted quickly away from their feet and the hosts of butterflies of all kinds that hovered and fluttered. Anne loved the little blue ones best and made up her mind to ask Mr Luffy what all their names were.

They had their lunch on a hill-top overlooking a vast stretch of heather, with grey-white blobs in it here and there – the sheep that wandered everywhere.

And, in the very middle of the meal, Anne heard the same rumbling she had heard before, and then, not far off, out spouted some white smoke from the ground. George went quite pale. Timmy leapt to his feet, growling and barking, his tail down. The boys roared with laughter.

'It's all right, Anne and George. It's only the trains underground here. We knew they ran under the moors and we thought we'd see what you did when you first heard them rumbling, and saw the smoke.'

'I'm not a bit frightened,' said Anne, and the boys looked at her, astonished. It was George who was the scared one! Usually it was quite the other way round.

George got back her colour and laughed. She called Timmy. 'It's all right, Tim. Come here. You know what trains are, don't you?'

The children discussed the trains. It really did seem strange to think of trains in those hollowed-out tunnels down below the moors – the people in them, reading their newspapers and talking – down in tunnels where the sun never shone at all.

'Come on,' said Julian, at last. 'Let's go on. We'll walk to the top of the next slope, and then I think we ought to turn back.'

They found a little path that Julian said must be a rabbit-path, because it was so narrow, and set off, chattering and laughing. They climbed through the heather to the top of the next slope. And at the top they got quite a surprise.

Down in the valley below was a silent and deserted stretch of railway lines! They appeared out of the black hole of a tunnel-mouth, ran for about half a mile, and then ended in what seemed to be a kind of railway yard.

'Look at that,' said Julian. 'Old derelict lines – not used any more, I should think. I suppose that tunnel's out of date, too.'

'Let's go down and have a squint,' said Dick. 'Come on! We've got plenty of time, and we can easily go back a shorter way.'

They set off down the hill to the lines. They arrived some way from the tunnel-mouth, and followed the lines to the deserted railway yard. There seemed to be nobody about at all.

'Look,' said Dick, 'there are some old wagons on that set of lines over there. They look as if they haven't been used for a hundred years. Let's give them a shove and set them going!'

'Oh, no!' said Anne, afraid. But the two boys and George, who had always longed to play about with real railway trucks, ran over to where three or four stood on the lines. Dick and Julian shoved hard at one. It moved. It ran a little way and crashed into the buffers of another. It made a terrific noise in the silent yard.

A door flew open in a tiny hut at the side of

the yard, and a terrifying figure came out. It was a one-legged man, with a wooden peg for his other leg, two great arms that might quite well belong to a gorilla, and a face as red as a tomato, except where grey whiskers grew.

He opened his mouth and the children expected a loud and angry yell. Instead out came a husky, hoarse whisper:

'What you doing? Ain't it bad enough to hear spook-trains a-running at night, without hearing them in the daytime, too?'

The four children stared at him. They thought he must be quite mad. He came nearer to them, and his wooden leg tip-tapped oddly. He swung his great arms loosely. He peered at the children as if he could hardly see them.

'I've broken me glasses,' he said, and to their astonishment and dismay two tears ran down his cheeks. 'Poor old Wooden-Leg Sam, he's broken his glasses. Nobody cares about Wooden-Leg Sam now, nobody at all.'

There didn't seem anything to say to all this.

Anne felt sorry for the funny old man, but she kept well behind Julian.

Sam peered at them again. 'Haven't you got tongues in your heads? Am I seeing things again, or are you there?'

'We're here and we're real,' said Julian. 'We happened to see this old railway yard and we came down to have a look at it. Who are you?'

'I told you – I'm Wooden-Leg Sam,' said the old man impatiently. 'The watchman, see? Though what there is to watch here, beats me. Do they think I'm going to watch for these spook-trains? Well, I'm not. Not me, Sam Wooden-Leg. I've seen many strange things in my life, yes, and been scared by them too, and I'm not watching for any more spook-trains.'

The children listened curiously. 'What spook-trains?' asked Julian.

Wooden-Leg Sam came closer. He looked all round as if he thought there might be someone listening, and then spoke in a hoarser whisper than usual.

'Spook-trains, I tell you. Trains that come out of that tunnel at night all by themselves, and go back all by themselves. Nobody in them. One night they'll come for old Sam Wooden-Leg – but, see, I'm smart, I am. I lock myself into my hut and get under the bed. And I blow my candle out so those spook-trains don't know I'm there.'

Anne shivered. She pulled at Julian's hand. 'Julian! Let's go. I don't like it. It sounds all peculiar and horrid. What does he mean?'

The old man seemed suddenly to change his mood. He picked up a large cinder and threw it at Dick, hitting him on the head. 'You clear out! I'm watchman here. And what did They tell me? They told me to chase away anyone that came. Clear out, I tell you!'

In terror Anne fled away. Timmy growled and would have leapt at the strange old watch-man, but George had her hand on his collar. Dick rubbed his head where the cinder had hit him.

'We're going,' he said soothingly to Sam. It

was plain that the old fellow was a bit funny in the head. 'We didn't mean to trespass. You look after your spook-trains. We won't interfere with you!'

The boys and George turned away, and caught up with Anne. 'What did he mean?' she asked, scared. 'What are spook-trains? Trains that aren't real? Does he really see them at night?'

'He just imagines them,' said Julian. 'I expect being there all alone in that deserted old railway yard has made him think strange things. Don't worry, Anne. There are no such things as spook-trains.'

'But he spoke as if there were,' said Anne, 'he really did. I'd hate to see a spook-train. Wouldn't you, Ju?'

'No. I'd *love* to see one,' said Julian, and he turned to Dick. 'Wouldn't you, Dick? Shall we come one night and watch? Just to see?'

[5]

Back at camp again

The children and Timmy left the deserted railway yard behind them and climbed up the heathery slope to find their way back to their camping-place. The boys could not stop talking about Wooden-Leg Sam and the strange things he said.

'It's a funny business altogether,' said Julian. 'I wonder why that yard isn't used any more – and where that tunnel leads to – and if trains ever do run there.'

'I expect there's quite an ordinary explanation,' said Dick. 'It's just that Wooden-Leg Sam made it all seem so weird. If there had been a proper watchman we shouldn't have thought there was anything strange about it at all.'

'Perhaps the boy at the farm would know,' said Julian. 'We'll ask him tomorrow. I'm afraid there aren't any spook-trains really – but, gosh, I'd love to go and watch for one, if there were any.'

'I wish you wouldn't talk like that,' said Anne, unhappily. 'You know, it makes me feel as if you want another adventure. And I don't.'

'Well, there won't be any adventure, so don't worry,' said Dick, comfortingly. 'And, anyway, if there was an adventure you could always go and hold old Luffy's hand. He wouldn't see an adventure if it was right under his nose. You'd be quite safe with him.'

'Look – who's that up there?' said George, seeing Timmy prick up his ears, and then hearing him give a little growl.

'Shepherd or something, I should think,' said Julian. He shouted out cheerfully. 'Good-afternoon! Nice day it's been!'

The old man on the path just above them nodded his head. He was either a shepherd or farm labourer of some sort. He waited for them to come up.

'Have you seen any of my sheep down along

there?' he asked them. 'They've got red crosses on them.'

'No. There aren't any down there,' said Julian. 'But there are some further along the hill. We've been down to the railway yard and we'd have seen any sheep on the slope below.'

'Don't you go down there,' said the old shepherd, his faded blue eyes looking into Julian's. 'That's a bad place, that is.'

'Well, we've been hearing about spook-trains!' said Julian, with a laugh. 'Is that what you mean?'

'Ay. There're trains that nobody knows of running out of that tunnel,' said the shepherd. 'Many's the time I've heard them when I've been up here at night with my sheep. That tunnel hasn't been used for thirty years – but the trains, they still come out of it, just as they used to.'

'How do you know? Have you seen them?' asked Julian, a cold shiver creeping down his spine quite suddenly.

'No. I've only heard them,' said the old man. 'Choo, choo, they go, and they jangle and clank. But they don't whistle any more. Old Wooden-Leg Sam reckons they're spook-trains, with nobody to drive them and nobody to tend them. Don't you go down to that place. It's bad and scary.'

Julian caught sight of Anne's scared face. He laughed loudly. 'What a tale! I don't believe in spook-trains – and neither do you, shepherd. Dick, have you got the tea in your bag? Let's find a nice place and have some sandwiches and cake. Will you join us, shepherd?'

'No, thank you kindly,' said the old man, moving off. 'I'll be after my sheep. Always wandering they are, and they keep me wandering, too. Good-day, and don't go down to that bad place.'

Julian found a good spot out of sight of 'that bad place', and they all sat down. 'All a lot of nonsense,' said Julian, who wanted Anne to feel happier again. 'We can easily ask the farmer's boy about it tomorrow. I expect it's all a silly tale made up by that old one-legged fellow, and passed on to the shepherd.'

'I expect so,' said Dick. 'You noticed that the shepherd had never actually *seen* the trains, Julian? Only heard them. Well, sound travels far at night, and I expect what he heard was simply the rumblings of the trains that go underground here. There's one going somewhere now! I can feel the ground trembling!'

They all could. It was a peculiar feeling. The rumbling stopped at last and they sat and ate their tea, watching Timmy scraping at a rabbit-hole and trying his hardest to get down it. He covered them with sandy soil as he burrowed, and nothing would stop him. He seemed to have gone completely deaf.

'Look here, if we don't get Timmy out of that hole now he'll be gone down so far that we'll have to drag him out by his tail,' said Julian, getting up. 'Timmy! TIM-MY! The rabbit's miles away. Come on out.'

It took both George and Julian to get him out. He was most indignant. He looked at them as if to say: '*Well*, what spoil-sports! Almost got him and you drag me out!'

He shook himself, and bits of grit and sand flew out of his hair. He took a step towards the hole again, but George caught hold of his tail. 'No, Timmy. Home now!'

'He's looking for a spook-train,' said Dick, and that made everyone laugh, even Anne.

They set off back to the camping-place, pleasantly tired, with Timmy following rather sulkily at their heels. When they at last got back they saw Mr Luffy sitting waiting for them. The blue smoke from his pipe curled up into the air.

'Hallo, hallo!' he said, and his brown eyes looked up at them from under his shaggy eyebrows. 'I was beginning to wonder if you'd got lost. Still, I suppose that dog of yours would always bring you back.'

Timmy wagged his tail politely. 'Woof,' he agreed, and went to drink out of the bucket of water. Anne stopped him just in time.

'No, Timmy! You're not to drink out of our washing-up water. There's yours, in the dish over there.'

Timmy went to his dish and lapped. He thought Anne was very fussy. Anne asked Mr Luffy if he would like any supper.

'We're not having a proper supper,' she said. 'We had tea so late. But I'll cook you something if you like, Mr Luffy.'

'Very kind of you. But I've had an enormous tea,' said Mr Luffy. 'I've brought up a fruit cake for you, from my own larder. Shall we share it for supper? And I've got a bottle of lime juice, too, which will taste grand with some of the stream water.'

The boys went off to get some fresh stream water for drinking. Anne got out some plates and cut slices of the cake.

'Well,' said Mr Luffy. 'Had a nice walk?'

'Yes,' said Anne, 'except that we met a strange one-legged man who told us he saw spook-trains.'

Mr Luffy laughed. 'Well, well! He must be a

cousin of a little girl I know who thought she was sitting on a volcano.'

Anne giggled. 'You're not to tease me. No, honestly, Mr Luffy, this old man was a watchman at a sort of old railway yard – not used now – and he said when the spook-trains came, he blew out his light and got under his bed so that they shouldn't get him.'

'Poor old fellow,' said Mr Luffy. 'I hope he didn't frighten you.'

'He did a bit,' said Anne. 'And he threw a cinder at Dick and hit him on the head. To-morrow we're going to the farm to ask the boy there if he's heard of the spook-trains, too. We met an old shepherd who said he'd heard them but not seen them.'

'Well, well – it all sounds most interesting,' said Mr Luffy. 'But these exciting stories usually have a very tame explanation, you know. Now would you like to see what I found today? A very rare and interesting little beetle.'

He opened a small square tin and showed a shiny beetle to Anne. It had green feelers and a red fiery spot near its tail-end. It was a lovely little thing.

'Now that's much more exciting to me than half a dozen spook-trains,' he told Anne. 'Spook-trains won't keep me awake at night – but thinking of this little beetle-fellow here certainly will.'

'I don't very much like beetles,' said Anne. 'But this one certainly is pretty. Do you really like hunting about all day for insects, and watching them, Mr Luffy?'

'Yes, very much,' said Mr Luffy. 'Ah, here come the boys with the water. Now we'll hand the cake round, shall we? Where's George? Oh, there she is, changing her shoes.'

George had a blister, and she had been putting a strip of plaster on her heel. She came up when the boys arrived and the cake was handed round. They sat in a circle, munching, while the sun gradually went down in a blaze of red.

'Nice day tomorrow again,' said Julian. 'What shall we do?'

'We'll have to go to the farm first,' said Dick.

'The farmer's wife said she'd let us have some more bread if we turned up in the morning. And we could do with more eggs if we can get them. We took eight hard-boiled ones with us today and we've only one or two left. And who's eaten all the tomatoes, I'd like to know?'

'All of you,' said Anne at once. 'You're perfect pigs over the tomatoes.'

'I'm afraid I'm one of the pigs,' apologised Mr Luffy. 'I think you fried me six for my breakfast, Anne.'

'That's all right,' said Anne. 'You didn't have as many as the others, even so! We can easily get some more.'

It was pleasant sitting there, eating and talking, and drinking lime juice and stream water. They were all tired, and it was nice to think of the cosy sleeping-bags. Timmy lifted his head and gave a vast yawn, showing an enormous amount of teeth.

'Timmy! I could see right down to your tail then!' said George. 'Do shut your mouth up. You've made us all yawn.'

So he had. Even Mr Luffy was yawning. He got up. 'Well, I'm going to turn in,' he said. 'Good-night. We'll make plans tomorrow morning. I'll bring up some breakfast for you, if you like. I've got some tins of sardines.'

'Oh, thanks,' said Anne. 'And there's some of this cake left. I hope you won't think that's too funny a breakfast, Mr Luffy – sardines and fruit cake?'

'Not a bit. It sounds a most sensible meal,' came Mr Luffy's voice from down the hillside. 'Good-night!'

The children sat there a few minutes longer. The sun went right out of sight. The wind grew a little chilly. Timmy yawned enormously again.

'Come on,' said Julian. 'Time we turned in. Thank goodness Timmy didn't come into our tent and walk all over me last night. Good-night, girls. It's going to be a heavenly night – but as I shall be asleep in about two shakes of a duck's tail, I shan't see much of it!'

The girls went into their tent. They were soon in their sleeping-bags. Just before they went to sleep Anne felt the slight shivering of the earth that meant a train was running underground somewhere. She could hear no rumbling sound. She fell asleep thinking of it.

The boys were not asleep. They, too, had felt the trembling of the earth beneath them, and it had reminded them of the old railway yard.

'Funny about those spook-trains, Dick,' said Julian, sleepily. 'Wonder if there *is* anything in it?'

'No. How could there be?' said Dick. 'All the same we'll go to the farm tomorrow and have a chat with that boy. He lives on the moors and he ought to know the truth.'

'The real truth is that Wooden-Leg Sam is potty, and imagines all he says, and the old shepherd is ready to believe in anything strange,' said Julian.

'I expect you're right,' said Dick. 'Oh my goodness, what's that?'

A dark shape stood looking in at the tent-flap. It gave a little whine.

'Oh, it's you, Timmy. Would you mind *not* coming and pretending you're a spook-train or something?' said Dick. 'And if you dare to put so much as half a paw on my middle, I'll scare you down the hill with a roar like a man-eating tiger. Go away.'

Timmy put a paw on Julian. Julian yelled out to George. 'George! Call this dog of yours, will you? He's just about to turn himself round twenty times on my middle, and curl himself up for the night.'

There was no answer from George. Timmy, feeling that he was not wanted, disappeared. He went back to George and curled himself up on her feet. He put his nose down on his paws and slept.

'Spooky Timmy,' murmured Julian, re-arranging himself. 'Timmy spooky – no, I mean – oh dear, what do I mean?'

'Shut up,' said Dick. 'What with you and Timmy messing about, I can't get – to – sleep!' But he could and he did – almost before he had finished speaking. Silence fell on the little camp, and nobody noticed when the next train rumbled underground – not even Timmy!

[6]
Day at the farm

The next day the children were up very early, as early as Mr Luffy, and they all had breakfast together. Mr Luffy had a map of the moorlands, and he studied it carefully after breakfast.

'I think I'll go off for the whole day,' he said to Julian, who was sitting beside him. 'See that little valley marked here – Crowleg Vale – well, I have heard that there are some of the rarest beetles in Britain to be found there. I think I'll take my gear and go along. What are you four going to do?'

'Five,' said George at once. 'You've forgotten Timmy.'

'So I have. I beg his pardon,' said Mr Luffy, solemnly. 'Well – what are you going to do?'

'We'll go over to the farm and get more

food,' said Julian. 'And ask that farm-boy if he's heard the tale of the spook-trains. And perhaps look round the farm and get to know the animals there. I always like a farm.'

'Right,' said Mr Luffy, beginning to light his pipe. 'Don't worry about me if I'm not back till dusk. When I'm bug-hunting I lose count of the time.'

'You're sure you won't get lost?' said Anne, anxiously. She didn't really feel that Mr Luffy could take proper care of himself.

'Oh yes. My right ear always warns me if I'm losing my way,' said Mr Luffy. 'It waggles hard.'

He waggled it at Anne and she laughed. 'I wish you'd tell me how you do that,' she said. 'I'm sure you know. You can't think how thrilled the girls at school would be if I learnt that trick. They'd think it was super.'

Mr Luffy grinned and got up. 'Well, so long,' he said. 'I'm off before Anne makes me give her a lesson in ear-waggles.'

He went off down the slope to his own tent.

George and Anne washed up, while the boys tightened some tent ropes that had come loose, and generally tidied up.

'I suppose it's quite all right leaving everything unguarded like this,' said Anne, anxiously.

'Well, we did yesterday,' said Dick. 'And who's likely to come and take anything up here in this wild and lonely spot, I'd like to know? You don't imagine a spook-train will come along and bundle everything into its luggage-van, do you, Anne?'

Anne giggled. 'Don't be silly. I just wondered if we ought to leave Timmy on guard, that's all.'

'Leave Timmy!' said George, amazed. 'You don't really think I'd leave Timmy behind every time we go off anywhere, Anne? Don't be an idiot.'

'No, I didn't really think you would,' said Anne. 'Well, I suppose nobody will come along here. Throw over that tea-cloth, George, if you've finished with it.'

Soon the tea-cloths were hanging over the

gorse bushes to dry in the sun. Everything was put away neatly in the tents. Mr Luffy had called a loud goodbye and gone. Now the five were ready to go off to the farm.

Anne took a basket, and gave one to Julian too. 'To bring back the food,' she said. 'Are you ready to go now?'

They set off over the heather, their knees brushing through the honeyed flowers, and sending scores of busy bees into the air. It was a lovely day again, and the children felt free and happy.

They came to the trim little farm. Men were at work in the fields, but Julian did not think they were very industrious. He looked about for the farm-boy.

The boy came out of a shed and whistled to them. 'Hallo! You come for some more eggs? I've collected quite a lot for you.'

He stared at Anne. 'You didn't come yesterday. What's your name?'

'Anne,' said Anne. 'What's yours?'

'Jock,' said the boy, with a grin. He was

rather a nice boy, Anne thought, with straw-coloured hair, blue eyes, and rather a red face which looked very good-tempered.

'Where's your mother?' said Julian. 'Can we get some bread and other things from her to-day? We ate an awful lot of our food yesterday, and we want to stock up our larder again!'

'She's busy just now in the dairy,' said Jock. 'Are you in a hurry? Come and see my pups.'

They all walked off with him to a shed. In there, right at the end, was a big box lined with straw. A collie dog lay there with five lovely little puppies. She growled at Timmy fiercely, and he backed hurriedly out of the shed. He had met fierce mother-dogs before, and he didn't like them!

The four children exclaimed over the fat little puppies, and Anne took one out very gently. It cuddled into her arms and made funny little whining noises.

'I wish it was mine,' said Anne. 'I should call it Cuddle.'

'What a frightful name for a dog,' said

George scornfully. 'Just the kind of silly name you *would* think of, Anne. Let me hold it. Are they all yours, Jock?'

'Yes,' said Jock, proudly. 'The mother's mine, you see. Her name's Biddy.'

Biddy pricked up her ears at her name and looked up at Jock out of bright, alert eyes. He fondled her silky head.

'I've had her for four years,' he said. 'When we were at Owl Farm, old Farmer Burrows gave her to me when she was eight weeks old.'

'Oh – were you at another farm before this one, then?' asked Anne. 'Have you always lived on a farm? Aren't you lucky!'

'I've only lived on two,' said Jock. 'Owl Farm and this one. Mum and I had to leave Owl Farm when Dad died, and we went to live in a town for a year. I hated that. I was glad when we came here.'

'But I thought your father was here!' said Dick, puzzled.

'That's my stepfather,' said Jock. 'He's no farmer, though!' He looked round and lowered his voice. 'He doesn't know much about farming. It's my mother that tells the men what to do. Still, he gives her plenty of money to do everything well, and we've got fine machinery and wagons and things. Like to see the dairy? It's slap up-to-date and Mum loves working in it.'

Jock took the four children to the shining, spotless dairy. His mother was at work there with a girl. She nodded and smiled at the children. 'Good-morning! Hungry again? I'll pack you up plenty of food when I've finished in the dairy. Would you like to stay and have dinner with my Jock? He's lonely enough here in the holidays, with no other boy to keep him company.'

'Oh, *yes* – do let's!' cried Anne, in delight. 'I'd like that. Can we, Ju?'

'Yes. Thank you very much, Mrs – er – Mrs . . .' said Julian.

'I'm Mrs Andrews,' said Jock's mother. 'But Jock is Jock Robins – he's the son of my first husband, a farmer. Well, stay to dinner all of you, and I'll see if I can give you a meal that will keep you going for the rest of the day!'

This sounded good. The four children felt thrilled, and Timmy wagged his tail hard. He liked Mrs Andrews.

'Come on,' said Jock, joyfully. 'I'll take you all round the farm, into every corner. It's not very big, but we're going to make it the best little farm on the moorlands. My stepfather doesn't seem to take much interest in the work of the farm, but he's jolly generous when it comes to handing out money to Mum to buy everything she wants.'

It certainly seemed to the children that the machinery on the farm was absolutely up-to-date. They examined the combine, they went into the little cowshed and admired the clean stone floor with white brick walls, they climbed into the red-painted wagons, and they wished they could try the two motor-tractors that stood side by side in a barn.

'You've got plenty of men here to work the farm,' said Julian. 'I shouldn't have thought there was enough for so many to do on this small place.'

'They're not good workers,' said Jock, his face creasing into frowns. 'Mum's always getting wild with them. They just don't know what to do. Dad gives her plenty of men to work the farm, but he always chooses the wrong ones! They don't seem to like farm-work, and they're always running off to the nearest town whenever they can. There's only one good fellow and he's old. See him over there? His name's Will.'

The children looked at Will. He was working in the little vegetable garden, an old fellow with a shrivelled face, a tiny nose and a pair of very blue eyes. They liked the look of him.

'Yes. He *looks* like a farm-worker,' said Julian. 'The others don't.'

'He won't work with them,' said Jock. 'He just says rude things to them, and calls them ninnies and idjits.'

'What's an idjit?' asked Anne.

'An idiot, silly,' said Dick. He walked up to old Will. 'Good-morning,' he said. 'You're very busy. There's always a lot to do on a farm, isn't there?'

The old fellow looked at Dick out of his very blue eyes, and went on with his work. 'Plenty to do and plenty of folk to do it, and not much done,' he said, in a croaking kind of voice. 'Never thought I'd be put to work with ninnies and idjits. Not ninnies and idjits!'

'There! What did I tell you?' said Jock, with a grin. 'He's always calling the other men that, so we just have to let him work right away from them. Still, I must say he's about right – most of the fellows here don't know the first thing about work on a farm. I wish my stepfather would let us have a few proper workers instead of these fellows.'

'Where's your stepfather?' said Julian, thinking he must be rather peculiar to pour money into a little moorland farm like this, and yet choose the wrong kind of workers.

'He's away for the day,' said Jock. 'Thank goodness!' he added, with a sideways look at the others.

'Why? Don't you like him?' asked Dick.

'He's all right,' said Jock. 'But he's not a farmer, though he makes out he's always wanted to be – and what's more he doesn't like me one bit. I try to like him for Mum's sake. But I'm always glad when he's out of the way.'

'Your mother's nice,' said George.

'Oh, yes – Mum's grand,' said Jock. 'You don't know what it means to her to have a little farm of her own again, and to be able to run it with the proper machinery and all.'

They came to a large barn. The door was locked. 'I told you what was in here before,' said Jock. 'Lorries! You can peek through that hole here at them. Don't know why my step-father wanted to buy up so many, but I suppose he got them cheap – he loves to get things cheap and sell them dear! He did say they'd be useful on the farm, to take goods to the market.'

'Yes – you told us that when we were here yesterday,' said Dick. 'But you've got heaps of wagons for that!'

'Yes. I reckon they weren't bought for the

farm at all, but for holding here till prices went high and he could make a lot of money,' said Jock, lowering his voice. 'I don't tell Mum that. So long as she gets what she wants for the farm, I'm going to hold my tongue.'

The children were very interested in all this. They wished they could see Mr Andrews. He must be a peculiar sort of fellow, they thought. Anne tried to imagine what he was like.

'Big and tall and dark and frowny,' she thought. 'Rather frightening and impatient, and he certainly won't like children. People like that never do.'

They spent a very pleasant morning poking about the little farm. They went back to see Biddy the collie and her pups. Timmy stood patiently outside the shed, with his tail down. He didn't like George to take so much interest in other dogs.

A bell rang loudly. 'Good! Dinner!' said Jock. 'We'd better wash. We're all filthy. Hope you feel hungry, because I guess Mum's got a super dinner for us.'

'I feel terribly hungry,' said Anne. 'It seems ages since we had breakfast. I've almost forgotten it!'

They all felt the same. They went into the farmhouse and were surprised to find a very nice little bathroom to wash in. Mrs Andrews was there, putting out a clean roller towel.

'Fine little bathroom, isn't it?' she said. 'My husband had it put in for me. First proper bathroom I've ever had!'

A glorious smell rose up from the kitchen downstairs. 'Come on!' said Jock, seizing the soap. 'Let's hurry. We'll be down in a minute, Mum!'

And they were. Nobody was going to dawdle over washing when a grand meal lay waiting for them downstairs!

Mr Andrews comes home

They all sat down to dinner. There was a big meat-pie, a cold ham, salad, potatoes in their jackets, and home-made pickles. It really was difficult to know what to choose.

'Have some of both,' said Mrs Andrews, cutting the meat-pie. 'Begin with the pie and go on with the ham. That's the best of living on a farm, you know – you do get plenty to eat.'

After the first course there were plums and thick cream, or jam tarts and the same cream. Everyone tucked in hungrily.

'I've never had such a lovely dinner in my life,' said Anne, at last. 'I wish I could eat some more but I can't. It was super, Mrs Andrews.'

'Smashing,' said Dick. That was his favourite word these holidays. 'Absolutely smashing.'

'Woof,' said Timmy, agreeing. He had had a

fine plateful of meaty bones, biscuits and gravy, and he had licked up every crumb and every drop. Now he felt he would like to have a snooze in the sun and not do a thing for the rest of the day.

The children felt rather like that, too. Mrs Andrews handed them a chocolate each and sent them out of doors. 'You go and have a rest now,' she said. 'Talk to Jock. He doesn't get enough company of his own age in the holidays. You can stay on to tea, if you like.'

'Oh thanks,' said everyone, although they all felt that they wouldn't even be able to manage a biscuit. But it was so pleasant at the farm that they felt they would like to stay as long as they could.

'May we borrow one of Biddy's puppies to have with us?' asked Anne.

'If Biddy doesn't mind,' said Mrs Andrews, beginning to clear away. 'And if Timmy doesn't eat it up!'

'Timmy wouldn't dream of it!' said George at once. 'You go and get the puppy, Anne. We'll find a nice place in the sun.'

Anne went off to get the puppy. Biddy didn't seem to mind a bit. Anne cuddled the fat little thing against her, and went off to the others, feeling very happy. The boys had found a fine place against a haystack, and sat leaning against it, the sun shining down warmly on them.

'Those men of yours seem to take a jolly good lunch-hour off,' said Julian, not seeing any of them about.

Jock gave a snort. 'They're bone lazy. I'd sack the lot if I were my stepfather. Mum's told him how badly the men work, but he doesn't say a word to them. I've given up bothering. I don't pay their wages – if I did, I'd sack the whole lot!'

'Let's ask Jock about the spook-trains,' said George, fondling Timmy's ears. 'It would be fun to talk about them.'

'Spook-trains? Whatever are they?' asked Jock, his eyes wide with surprise. 'Never heard of them!'

'Haven't you really?' asked Dick. 'Well, you don't live very far from them, Jock!'

'Tell me about them,' said Jock. 'Spook-trains – no, I've never heard of one of those.'

'Well, I'll tell you what we know,' said Julian. 'Actually we thought you'd be able to tell us much more about them than we know ourselves.'

He began to tell Jock about their visit to the deserted railway yard, and Wooden-Leg Sam, and his peculiar behaviour. Jock listened, enthralled.

'Coo! I wish I'd been with you. Let's all go there together, shall we?' he said. 'This was quite an adventure you had, wasn't it? You know, I've never had a single adventure in all my life, not even a little one. Have you?'

The four children looked at one another, and Timmy looked at George. Adventures! What didn't they know about them? They had had so many.

'Yes. We've had heaps of adventures – real ones – smashing ones,' said Dick. 'We've been down in dungeons, we've been lost in caves, we've found secret passages, we've looked for treasure – well, I can't tell you what we've done! It would take too long.'

'No, it wouldn't,' said Jock eagerly. 'You tell me. Go on. Did you all have the adventures? Little Anne, here, too?'

'Yes, all of us,' said George. 'And Timmy as well. He rescued us heaps of times from danger. Didn't you, Tim?'

'Woof, woof,' said Timmy, and thumped his tail against the hay.

They began to tell Jock about their many adventures. He was a very, very good listener. His eyes almost fell out of his head, and he went brick-red whenever they came to an exciting part.

'My word!' he said at last. 'I've never heard such things in my life before. Aren't you lucky? You just go about having adventures all the time, don't you? I *say* – do you think you'll have one here, these hols?'

Julian laughed. 'No. Whatever kind of adventure would there be on these lonely moorlands? Why, you yourself have lived here for three years, and haven't even had a tiny adventure.'

Jock sighed. 'That's true. I haven't.' Then his eyes brightened again. 'But see here – what about those spook-trains you've been asking me about? Perhaps you'll have an adventure with those?'

'Oh, no, I don't want to,' said Anne, in a horrified voice. 'An adventure with spook-trains would be simply horrid.'

'I'd like to go down to that old railway yard with you and see Wooden-Leg Sam,' said Jock longingly. 'Why, that would be a real adventure to me, you know – just talking to a funny old man like that, and wondering if he was suddenly going to throw cinders at us. Take me with you next time you go.'

'Well – I don't know that we meant to go again,' said Julian. 'There's really nothing much in his story except imagination – the old watchman's gone peculiar in the head through being alone there so much, guarding a yard where nothing and nobody ever comes. He's just remembering the trains that used to go in and out before the line was given up.'

'But the shepherd said the same as Sam,' said Jock. 'I *say* – what about going down there one night and watching for a spook-train!'

'NO!' said Anne, in horror.

'You needn't come,' said Jock. 'Just us three boys.'

'And me,' said George at once. 'I'm as good as any boy, and I'm not going to be left out. Timmy's coming, too.'

'Oh, please don't make these awful plans,' begged poor Anne. 'You'll *make* an adventure come, if you go on like this.'

Nobody took the least notice of her. Julian looked at Jock's excited face. 'Well,' he said, 'if we do go there again, we'll tell you. And if we think we'll go watching for spook-trains, we'll take you with us.'

Jock looked as if he could hug Julian. 'That would be terrific,' he said. 'Thanks a lot. Spook-trains! I *say*, just suppose we really did see one! Who'd be driving it? Where would it come from?'

'Out of the tunnel, Wooden-Leg Sam says,' said Dick. 'But I don't see how we'd spot it, except by the noise it made, because apparently the spook-trains only arrive in the dark of the night. Never in the daytime. We wouldn't *see* much, even if we were there.'

It was such an exciting subject to Jock that he persisted in talking about it all the afternoon. Anne got tired of listening, and went to sleep with Biddy's puppy in her arms. Timmy curled up by George and went to sleep too. He wanted to go for a walk, but he could see that there was no hope with all this talking going on.

It was tea-time before any of them had expected it. The bell rang, and Jock looked most surprised.

'Tea! Would you believe it? Well, I *have* had an exciting afternoon talking about all this. And look here, if you don't make up your minds to go spook-train hunting I'll jolly well go off by myself. If only I could have an adventure like the kind you've had, I'd be happy.'

They went in to tea, after waking Anne up with difficulty. She took the puppy back to Biddy, who received it gladly and licked it all over.

Julian was surprised to find that he was quite hungry again. 'Well,' he said, as he sat down at the table, 'I didn't imagine I'd feel hungry again for a week – but I do. What a marvellous tea, Mrs Andrews. Isn't Jock lucky to have meals like this always!'

There were home-made scones with new honey. There were slices of bread thickly spread with butter, and new-made cream cheese to go with it. There was sticky brown gingerbread, hot from the oven, and a big solid fruit cake that looked almost like a plum pudding when it was cut, it was so black.

'Oh dear! I wish now I hadn't had so much dinner,' sighed Anne. 'I don't feel hungry enough to eat a bit of everything and I would so like to!'

Mrs Andrews laughed. 'You eat what you can, and I'll give you some to take away, too,' she said. 'You can have some cream cheese, and the scones and honey – and some of the bread I made this morning. And maybe you'd like a slab of the gingerbread. I made plenty.'

'Oh, thanks,' said Julian. 'We'll be all right tomorrow with all that. You're a marvellous cook, Mrs Andrews. I wish I lived on your farm.'

There was the sound of a car coming slowly up the rough track to the farmhouse, and Mrs Andrews looked up. 'That's Mr Andrews come back,' she said. 'My husband, you know, Jock's stepfather.'

Julian thought she looked a little worried. Perhaps Mr Andrews didn't like children and wouldn't be pleased to see them sitting round his table when he came home tired.

'Would you like us to go, Mrs Andrews?' he asked politely. 'Perhaps Mr Andrews would like a bit of peace for his meal when he comes in – and we're rather a crowd, aren't we?'

Jock's mother shook her head. 'No, you can stay. I'll get him a meal in the other room if he'd like it.'

Mr Andrews came in. He wasn't in the least like Anne or the others had imagined him to be. He was a short, dark little man, with a weak face and a nose much too big for it. He looked harassed and bad-tempered, and stopped short when he saw the five children.

'Hallo, dear,' said Mrs Andrews. 'Jock's got his friends here today. Would you like a bit of tea in your room? I can easily put a tray there.'

'Well,' said Mr Andrews, smiling a watery kind of smile, 'perhaps it would be best. I've had a worrying kind of day, and not much to eat.'

'I'll get you a tray of ham and pickles and bread,' said his wife. 'It won't take a minute. You go and wash.'

Mr Andrews went out. Anne was surprised that he seemed so small and looked rather stupid. She had imagined someone big and burly, strong and clever, who was always going about doing grand deals and making a lot of money. Well, he must be cleverer than he looked, to make enough money to give Mrs Andrews all she needed for her farm.

Mrs Andrews bustled about with this and that, laying a tray with a snow-white cloth, and plates of food. Mr Andrews could be heard in the bathroom, splashing as he washed. Then he came downstairs and put his head in at the door. 'My meal ready?' he asked. 'Well, Jock – had a good day?'

'Yes, thanks,' said Jock, as his stepfather took the tray from his mother and turned to go. 'We went all round the farm this morning – and we talked and talked this afternoon. And oh, I say – do you know anything about spook-trains, sir?'

Mr Andrews was just going out of the door. He turned in surprise. 'Spook-trains? What are you talking about?'

'Well, Julian says there's an old deserted railway yard a good way from here, and spook-trains are supposed to come out of the tunnel there in the dark of night,' said Jock. 'Have you heard of them?'

Mr Andrews stood stock still, his eyes on his stepson. He looked dismayed and shocked. Then he came back into the room and kicked the door shut behind him.

'I'll have my tea here after all,' he said. 'Well, to think you've heard of those spook-trains! I've been careful not to mention them to your mother or to you, Jock, for fear of scaring you!'

'Gee!' said Dick. 'Are they really true then? They can't be.'

'You tell me all you know, and how you know about it,' said Mr Andrews, sitting down at the table with his tray. 'Go on. Don't miss out a thing. I want to hear everything.'

Julian hesitated. 'Oh – there's nothing really to tell, sir – just a lot of nonsense.'

'You tell it me!' almost shouted Mr Andrews. 'Then I'll tell *you* a few things. And I tell you, you won't go near that old railway yard again – no, that you won't!'

[8]

A lazy evening

The five children and Mrs Andrews stared in surprise at Mr Andrews, when he shouted at them. He repeated some of his words again.

'Go on! You tell me all you know. And then I'll tell *you*!'

Julian decided to tell, very shortly, what had happened at the old railway yard, and what Wooden-Leg Sam had said. He made the tale sound rather bald and dull. Mr Andrews listened to it with the greatest interest, never once taking his eyes off Julian.

Then he sat back and drank a whole cup of strong tea in one gulp. The children waited for him to speak, wondering what he had to say.

'Now,' he said, making his voice sound important and impressive, 'you listen to me. Don't any of you ever go down to that yard again. It's a bad place.'

'Why?' asked Julian. 'What do you mean – a bad place?'

'Things have happened there – years and years ago,' said Mr Andrews. 'Bad things. Accidents. It was all shut up after that and the tunnel wasn't used any more. See? Nobody was allowed to go there, and nobody did, because they were scared. They knew it was a bad place, where bad things happen.'

Anne felt frightened. 'But Mr Andrews – you don't mean there really are spook-trains, do you?' she asked, her face rather pale.

Mr Andrews pursed up his lips and nodded very solemnly indeed. 'That's just what I do mean. Spook-trains come and go. Nobody knows why. But it's bad luck to be there when they come. They might take you away, see?'

Julian laughed. 'Oh – not as bad as that, sir, surely! Anyway, you're frightening Anne, so let's change the subject. I don't believe in spook-trains.'

But Mr Andrews didn't seem to want to stop talking about the trains. 'Wooden-Leg Sam was right to hide himself when they come along,' he said. 'I don't know how he manages to stay on in a bad place like that. Never knowing when a train is going to come creeping out of that tunnel in the darkness.'

Julian was not going to have Anne frightened any more. He got up from the table and turned to Mrs Andrews.

'Thank you very much for a lovely day and lovely food!' he said. 'We must go now. Come along, Anne.'

'Wait a minute,' said Mr Andrews. 'I just want to warn you all very solemnly that you mustn't go down to that railway yard. You hear me, Jock? You might never come back. Old Wooden-Leg Sam's mad, and well he may be, with spook-trains coming along in the dead of night. It's a bad and dangerous place. You're not to go near it!'

'Well – thank you for the warning, sir,' said Julian, politely, suddenly disliking the small man with the big nose very much indeed. 'We'll be going. Goodbye, Mrs Andrews. Goodbye, Jock. Come along tomorrow and have a picnic with us, will you?'

'Oh, thanks! Yes, I will,' said Jock. 'But wait a minute – aren't you going to take any food with you?'

'Yes, of course they are,' said Mrs Andrews, getting up from her chair. She had been listening to the conversation with a look of puzzled wonder on her face. She went out into the scullery, where there was a big, cold larder. Julian followed her. He carried the two baskets.

'I'll give you plenty,' said Mrs Andrews, putting loaves, butter, and cream cheese into the baskets. 'I know what appetites you youngsters get. Now don't you be too scared at what my husband's just been saying – I saw that little Anne was frightened. I've never heard of the spook-trains, and I've been here for three years. I don't reckon there's much in the tale, you know, for all my husband's so set on warning you not to go down to the yard.'

Julian said nothing. He thought that Mr Andrews had behaved rather oddly about the whole story. Was he one of the kind of people who believed in all sorts of silly things and got scared himself? He looked weak enough! Julian found himself wondering how a nice woman like Mrs Andrews could have married such a poor specimen of a man. Still, he was a generous fellow, judging by all Jock had said, and perhaps Jock's mother felt grateful to him for giving her the farm and the money to run it with. That must be it.

Julian thanked Mrs Andrews, and insisted on paying her, though she would have given him the food for nothing. She came into the kitchen with him and he saw that the others had already gone outside. Only Mr Andrews was left, eating ham and pickles.

'Goodbye, sir,' said Julian politely.

'Goodbye. And you remember what I've told you, boy,' said Mr Andrews. 'Bad luck comes to people who see the spook-trains – yes, terrible bad luck. You keep away from them.'

Julian gave a polite smile and went out. It was evening now and the sun was setting behind the moorland hills, though it still had a long way to go before it disappeared. He caught up with the others. Jock was with them.

'I'm just coming half-way with you,' said Jock. 'I say! My stepfather was pretty scary about those trains, wasn't he?'

'I felt pretty scary too, when he was warning us about them,' said Anne. 'I shan't go down to that yard again, ever. Will you, George?'

'If the boys did, I would,' said George, who didn't look very much as if she wanted to, all the same.

'*Are* you going to the yard again?' asked Jock, eagerly. 'I'm not scared. Not a bit. It would be an adventure to go and watch for a spook-train.'

'We might go,' said Julian. 'We'll take you with us, if we do. But the girls aren't to come.'

'Well, I like that!' said George angrily. 'As if you could leave me behind! When have I been scared of anything? I'm as brave as any of you.'

'Yes. I know. You can come as soon as we find out it's all a silly story,' said Julian.

'I shall come whenever you go,' flashed back George. 'Don't you dare to leave me out. I'll never speak to you again if you do.'

Jock looked most surprised at this sudden flare-up of temper from George. He didn't know how fierce she could be!

'I don't see why George shouldn't come,' he said. 'I bet she'd be every bit as good as a boy. I thought she was one when I first saw her.'

George gave him one of her sweetest smiles. He couldn't have said anything she liked better! But Julian would not change his mind.

'I mean what I say. The girls won't come if we do go, so that's that. For one thing, Anne certainly wouldn't want to come, and if George came without her she'd be left all alone up at the camp. She wouldn't like that.'

'She could have Mr Luffy's company,' said George, looking sulky again.

'Idiot! As if we'd want to tell Mr Luffy we were going off exploring deserted railway yards watched over by a mad, one-legged fellow who swears there are spook-trains!' said Julian. 'He'd stop us going. You know what grown-ups are like. Or he'd come with us, which would be worse.'

'Yes. He'd see moths all the time, not spook-trains,' said Dick, with a grin.

'I'd better go back now,' said Jock. 'It's been a grand day. I'll come up tomorrow and picnic with you. Goodbye.'

They called goodbye to Jock, and went on their way to the camp. It was quite nice to see it again, waiting for them, the two tents flapping a little in the breeze. Anne pushed her way through the tent-flap, anxious to see that every-thing was untouched.

Inside the tent it was very hot. Anne decided to put the food they had brought under the bottom of the big gorse bush. It would be cooler there. She was soon busy about her little jobs. The boys went down to see if Mr Luffy was back, but he wasn't.

'Anne! We're going to bathe in the stream!'

they called. 'We feel hot and dirty. Are you coming? George is coming too.'

'No, I won't come,' Anne called back. 'I've got lots of things to do.'

The boys grinned at one another. Anne did so enjoy 'playing house'. So they left her to it, and went to the stream, from which yells and howls and shrieks soon came. The water was colder than they expected, and nobody liked to lie down in it – but everyone was well and truly splashed, and the icy-cold drops falling on their hot bodies made them squeal and yell. Timmy didn't in the least mind the iciness of the water. He rolled over and over in it, enjoying himself.

'Look at him, showing off!' said Dick. 'Aha, Timmy, if I could bathe in a fur coat like you, I wouldn't mind the cold water either.'

'Woof,' said Timmy, and climbed up the shallow bank. He shook himself violently and thousands of icy-cold silvery drops flew from him and landed on the three shivering children. They yelled and chased him away.

It was a pleasant, lazy evening. Mr Luffy

didn't appear at all. Anne got a light meal of bread and cream cheese and a piece of ginger-bread. Nobody felt like facing another big meal that day. They lay in the heather and talked comfortably.

'This is the kind of holiday I like,' said Dick.

'So do I,' said Anne. 'Except for the spook-trains. That's spoilt it a bit for me.'

'Don't be silly, Anne,' said George. 'If they are not real it's just a silly story, and if they are real, well, it might be an adventure.'

There was a little silence. 'Are we going down to the yard again?' asked Dick lazily.

'Yes, I think so,' said Julian. 'I'm not going to be scared off it by weird warnings from Pa Andrews.'

'Then I vote we go one night and wait to see if a spook-train does come along,' said Dick.

'I shall come too,' said George.

'No, you won't,' said Julian. 'You'll stay with Anne.'

George said nothing, but everyone could feel mutiny in the air.

'Do we tell Mr Luffy, or don't we?' said Dick.

'You know we've said we wouldn't,' said Julian. He yawned. 'I'm getting sleepy. And the sun has gone, so it will soon be dark. I wonder where old Luffy is?'

'Do you think I'd better wait up and see if he wants something to eat?' said Anne, anxiously.

'No. Not unless you want to keep awake till midnight!' said Julian. 'He'll have got some food down in his tent. He'll be all right. I'm going to turn in. Coming, Dick?'

The boys were soon in their sleeping-bags. The girls lay in the heather for a little while longer, listening to the lonely-sounding cry of the curlews going home in the dusk. Then they, too, went into their own tent.

Once safely in their sleeping-bags, the two boys felt suddenly wide awake. They began to talk in low voices.

'Shall we take Jock down to see the yard in the daytime? Or shall we go one night and watch for the Train from Nowhere?' said Julian.

'I vote we go and watch at night,' said Dick. 'We'll never see a spook-train in the daytime. Wooden-Leg Sam is an interesting old chap, especially when he chucks cinders about – but I don't know that I like him enough to go and visit him again!'

'Well – if Jock badly wants to go and have a snoop round tomorrow morning when he comes, we'd better take him,' said Julian. 'We can always go one night, too, if we want to.'

'Right. We'll wait and see what Jock says,' said Dick. They talked a little longer and then felt sleepy. Dick was just dropping off when he heard something coming wriggling through the heather. A head was stuck through the opening of the tent.

'If you dare to come in, I'll smack your silly face,' said Dick, thinking it was Timmy. 'I know what you want, you perfect pest – you want to flop down on my tummy. You just turn yourself round and go away! Do you hear?'

The head in the opening moved a little but

didn't go away. Dick raised himself up on one elbow.

'Put one paw inside my tent and you'll be sent rolling down the hill!' he said. 'I love you very much in the daytime, but I'm not fond of you at night – not when I'm in a sleeping-bag anyway. Scoot!'

The head made a peculiar apologetic sound. Then it spoke. 'Er – you're awake, I see. Are all of you all right – the girls too? I'm only just back.'

'Gosh! It's Mr Luffy,' said Dick, filled with horror. I say, sir – I'm most awfully sorry – I thought you were Timmy, come to flop himself down on top of me, like he often does. So sorry, sir.'

'Don't mention it!' said the shadowy head with a chuckle. 'Glad you're all right. See you tomorrow!'

[9]

Night visitor

Mr Luffy slept very late the next morning and nobody liked to disturb him. The girls yelled with laughter when they heard how Dick had spoken to him the night before, thinking he was Timmy the dog.

'He was very decent about it,' said Dick. 'Seemed to think it was quite amusing. I hope he'll still think so this morning!'

They were all sitting eating their breakfast – ham, tomatoes, and the bread Mrs Andrews had given them the day before. Timmy collected the bits as usual, and wondered if George would let him have a lick of the cream cheese she was now putting on her bread. Timmy loved cheese. He looked at the lump in the dish and sighed all over George. He could easily eat that in one mouthful! How he wished he could.

'I wonder what time Jock will come up,' said George. 'If he came up pretty soon, we could go for a nice long walk over the moors, and picnic somewhere. Jock ought to know some fine walks.'

'Yes. We'll mess about till he comes, and then tell him he's to be our guide and take us to the nicest walk he knows,' said Anne. 'Oh Timmy, you beast – you've taken my nice lump of cream cheese right out of my fingers!'

'Well, you were waving it about under his nose, so what could you expect?' said George. 'He thought you were giving it to him.'

'Well, he shan't have any more. It's too precious,' said Anne. 'Oh, dear – I wish we didn't eat so much. We keep bringing in stacks of food, and it hardly lasts any time.'

'I bet Jock will bring some more,' said Dick. 'He's a sensible sort of fellow. Did you get a peep into that enormous larder of his mother's? It's like a great cave, goes right back into the wall, with dozens of stone shelves – and all filled with food. No wonder Jock's tubby.'

'Is he? I never noticed,' said Anne. 'Is that him whistling?'

It wasn't. It was a curlew, very high up. 'Too early for him yet,' said Julian. 'Shall we help you to clear up, Anne?'

'No. That's my job and George's,' said Anne firmly. 'You go down and see if Mr Luffy is awake. He can have a bit of ham and a few tomatoes, if he likes.'

They went down to Mr Luffy's tent. He was awake, sitting at the entrance, eating some kind of breakfast. He waved a sandwich at them.

'Hallo, there! I'm late this morning. I had a job getting back. I went much too far. Sorry I woke you up last night, Dick.'

'You didn't. I wasn't asleep,' said Dick, going rather red. 'Did you have a good day, Mr Luffy?'

'Bit disappointing. Didn't find quite all the creatures I'd hoped,' said Mr Luffy. 'What about you? Did you have a good day?'

'Fine,' said Dick, and described it. Mr Luffy seemed very interested in everything, even in

Mr Andrews's rather frightening warning about the railway yard.

'Silly chap he sounds,' said Mr Luffy, shaking the crumbs off his front. 'All the same – I should keep away from the yard, if I were you. Stories don't get about for nothing, you know. No smoke without fire!'

'Why, sir – surely *you* don't believe there's anything spooky about the trains there?' said Dick, in surprise.

'Oh, no – I doubt if there *are* any trains,' said Mr Luffy. 'But when a place has got a bad name it's usually best to keep away from it.'

'I suppose so, sir,' said Dick and Julian together. Then they hastily changed the subject, afraid that Mr Luffy, like Mr Andrews, might also be going to forbid them to visit the railway yard. And the more they were warned about it and forbidden to go, the more they felt that they really must!

'Well, we must get back,' said Dick. 'We're expecting Jock – that's the boy at the farm – to come up for the day, and we thought we'd go out walking and take our food with us. Are you going out, too, sir?'

'Not today,' said Mr Luffy. 'My legs are tired and stiff with so much scrambling about yesterday, and I want to mount some of the specimens I found. Also I'd like to meet your farm friend – what's his name – Jock?'

'Yes, sir,' said Julian. 'Right. We'll bring him along as soon as he comes, then off we'll go. You'll be left in peace all day!'

But Jock didn't come. The children waited for him all the morning and he didn't turn up. They held up their lunch until they were too hungry to wait any longer, and then they had it on the heather in front of their tents.

'Funny,' said Julian. 'He knows where the camp is, because we pointed it out to him when he came half-way home with us yesterday. Perhaps he'll come this afternoon.'

But he didn't come in the afternoon either, nor did he come after tea. Julian debated whether or not to go and see what was up, but decided against it. There must be some good reason why Jock hadn't come, and Mrs Andrews wouldn't want them all visiting her two days running.

It was a disappointing day. They didn't like to leave the tents and go for even a short stroll in case Jock came. Mr Luffy was busy all day long with his specimens. He was sorry Jock had disappointed them. 'He'll come tomorrow,' he said. 'Have you got enough food? There's some in that tin over there if you want it.'

'Oh, no thank you, sir,' said Julian. 'We've plenty really. We're going to have a game of cards. Like to join us?'

'Yes, I think I will,' said Mr Luffy, getting up and stretching himself. 'Can you play rummy?'

They could – and they beat poor Mr Luffy handsomely, because he couldn't play at all. He blamed his luck on his bad cards, but he enjoyed the game immensely. He said the only thing that really put him off was the way that Timmy stood behind him and breathed down his neck all the time.

'I kept feeling certain that Timmy thought he

knew how to play my cards better than I could,' he complained. 'And whenever I did something wrong, he breathed down my neck harder than usual.'

Everyone laughed, and George privately thought that Timmy would probably play very much better than Mr Luffy if only he could hold the cards.

Jock didn't come at all. They put the cards away when they could no longer see them, and Mr Luffy announced that he was going to bed. 'It was very late when I got back last night,' he said. 'I really must have an early night.'

The others thought they would go to bed too. The thought of their cosy sleeping-bags was always a nice one when darkness came on.

The girls crept into their bags and Timmy flopped down on George. The boys were in their bags about the same time and Dick gave a loud yawn.

'Good-night, Ju,' he said, and fell fast asleep. Julian was soon asleep too. In fact, everyone was sound asleep when Timmy gave a little growl. It was such a small growl that neither of the girls heard it, and certainly Dick and Julian didn't, away in their tent.

Timmy raised his head and listened intently. Then he gave another small growl. He listened again. Finally he got up, shook himself, still without waking George, and stalked out of the tent, his ears cocked and his tail up. He had heard somebody or something, and although he thought it was all right, he was going to make sure.

Dick was sound asleep when he felt something brushing against the outside of his tent. He awoke at once and sat up. He looked at the tent opening. A shadow appeared there and looked in.

Was it Timmy? Was it Mr Luffy? He mustn't make a mistake this time. He waited for the shadow to speak. But it didn't! It just stayed there as if it were listening for some movement inside the tent. Dick didn't like it.

'Timmy!' he said at last, in a low voice.

Then the shadow spoke: 'Dick? Or is it Julian? It's Jock here. I've got Timmy beside me. Can I come in?'

'*Jock*!' said Dick, in surprise. 'Whatever have you come at this time of night for? And why didn't you come today? We waited ages for you.'

'Yes, I know. I'm awfully sorry,' said Jock's voice, and the boy wriggled himself into the tent. Dick poked Julian awake.

'Julian! Here's Jock – and Timmy. Get off me, Timmy. Here, Jock, see if you can squeeze inside my sleeping-bag – there's room for us both, I think.'

'Oh, thanks,' said Jock, and squeezed inside with difficulty. 'How warm it is! I say, I'm terribly sorry I didn't come today – but my stepfather suddenly announced he wanted me to go somewhere with him for the whole day. Can't think why. He doesn't bother about me as a rule.'

'That was mean of him, seeing that he knew you were to come on a picnic with us,' said Julian. 'Was it something important?'

'No. Not at all,' said Jock. 'He drove off to Endersfield – that's about forty miles away –

parked me in the public library there, saying he'd be back in a few minutes – and he didn't come back till past tea-time! I had some sand-wiches with me, luckily. I felt pretty angry about it, I can tell you.'

'Never mind. Come tomorrow instead,' said Dick.

'I can't,' said Jock in despair. 'He's gone and arranged for me to meet the son of some friend of his – a boy called Cecil Dearlove – what a name! I'm to spend the day with this frightful boy. The worst of it is Mum's quite pleased about it. She never thinks my stepfather takes enough notice of me – good thing he doesn't, *I* think.'

'Oh blow – so you won't be able to come tomorrow either,' said Julian. 'Well – what about the next day?'

'It should be all right,' said Jock. 'But I've feeling I'll have dear love of a Cecil plonked on me for the day – to show him the cows and the puppies, dear pet! Ugh! When I could be with you four and Timmy.'

'It's bad luck,' said Julian. 'It really is.'

'I thought I'd better come and tell you,' said Jock. 'It's the first chance I've had, creeping up here tonight. I've brought some more food for you, by the way. I guessed you'd want some. I feel down in the dumps about that adventure – you know, going to see the railway yard. I was going to ask you to take me today.'

'Well – if you can't come tomorrow either – and perhaps not the next day – what about going one night?' said Dick. 'Would you like to come up tomorrow night, about this time? We won't tell the girls. We'll just go off by ourselves, we three boys – and watch!'

Jock was too thrilled to say a word. He let out a deep breath of joy. Dick laughed.

'Don't get too thrilled. We probably shan't see a thing. Bring a torch if you've got one. Come to our tent and jerk my toe. I'll probably be awake, but if I'm not, that'll wake me all right! And don't say a word to anyone of course.'

'Rather not,' said Jock, overjoyed. 'Well – I suppose I'd better be going. It was pretty weird coming over the moorland in the dark. There's no moon, and the stars don't give much light. I've left the food outside the tent. Better look out that Timmy doesn't get it.'

'Right. Thanks awfully,' said Julian. Jock got out of Dick's sleeping-bag and went backwards out of the tent, with Timmy obligingly licking his nose all the way. Jock then found the bag of food and rolled it in to Julian, who put it safely under the groundsheet.

'Goodnight,' said Jock, in a low voice, and they heard him scrambling over the heather. Timmy went with him, pleased at this unexpected visitor, and the chance of a midnight walk. Jock was glad to have the dog's company. Timmy went right to the farm with him and then bounded back over the moorland to the camping-place, longing to pounce on the rabbits he could smell here and there, but wanting to get back to George.

In the morning Anne was amazed to find the food in her 'larder' under the gorse bush. Julian had popped it there to surprise her. 'Look at this!' she cried, in astonishment. 'Meat-pies – more tomatoes – eggs, wherever did they come from?'

'Spook-train brought them in the night,' said Dick, with a grin.

'Volcano shot them up into the air,' said Mr Luffy, who was also there. Anne threw a tea-cloth at him.

'Tell me how it came here,' she demanded. 'I was worried about what to give you all for breakfast – and now there's more than we can possibly eat. Who put it there? George, do you know?'

But George didn't. She glanced at the smiling faces of the two boys. 'I bet Jock was here last night,' she said to them. 'Wasn't he?' And to herself she said: 'Yes – and somehow I think they've planned something together. You won't trick *me*, Dick and Julian. I'll be on the lookout from now on! Wherever you go, I go too!'

[10]

Hunt for a spook-train

That day passed pleasantly enough. The children, Timmy, and Mr Luffy all went off to a pool high up on the moorlands. It was called 'the Green Pool' because of its cucumber-green colour. Mr Luffy explained that some curious chemicals found there caused the water to look green.

'I hope we shan't come out looking green, too,' said Dick, getting into his bathing trunks. 'Are you going to bathe, Mr Luffy?'

Mr Luffy was. The children expected him to be a very poor swimmer and to splash about at the edge and do very little – but to their surprise he was magnificent in the water, and could swim faster even than Julian.

They had great fun, and when they were tired they came out to bask in the sun. The high road ran alongside the Green Pool, and the children watched a herd of sheep being driven along, then a car or two came by, and finally a big army lorry. A boy sat beside the driver, and to the children's surprise he waved wildly at them.

'Who was that?' said Julian astonished. 'Surely he doesn't know us?'

George's sharp eyes had seen who it was. 'It was Jock! Sitting beside the driver. And, look, here comes his stepfather's fine new car. Jock's preferred to go with the lorry-driver instead of his stepfather! I don't blame him, either!'

The bright new car came by, driven by Mr Andrews. He didn't glance at the children by the wayside, but drove steadily on after the lorry.

'Going to market, I suppose,' said Dick, lying back again. 'Wonder what they're taking?'

'So do I,' said Mr Luffy. 'He must sell his farm produce at very high prices to be able to buy that fine car and all the machinery and gear you've told me about. Clever fellow, Mr Andrews!'

'He doesn't look at all clever,' said Anne. 'He looks rather a weak, feeble sort of man, really, Mr Luffy. I can't even imagine him being clever enough to beat anyone down, or get the better of them.'

'Very interesting,' said Mr Luffy. 'Well, what about another dip before we have our dinner?'

It was a very nice day, and Mr Luffy was very good company. He could make fine jokes very solemnly indeed, and only the fact that his ear waggled violently showed the others that he too was enjoying the joke. His right ear seemed to love to join in the joke, even if Mr Luffy's face was as solemn as Timmy's.

They arrived home at the camp about tea-time and Anne got a fine tea ready. They took it down to eat in front of Mr Luffy's tent. As the evening came on Julian and Dick felt excitement rising in them. In the daytime neither of them really believed a word about the spook-trains, but as the sun sank and long shadows crept down the hills they felt pleasantly thrilled. Would they really see anything exciting that night?

It was a very dark night at first, because clouds lay across the sky and hid even the stars. The boys said good-night to the girls and snuggled down into their sleeping-bags. They watched the sky through the tent opening.

Gradually the big clouds thinned out. A few stars appeared. The clouds thinned still more and fled away in rags. Soon the whole sky was bright with pin-points of light, and a hundred thousand stars looked down on the moorlands.

'We shall have a bit of starlight to see by,' whispered Julian. 'That's good. I don't want to stumble about over the heather and break my ankle in rabbit-holes in the pitch darkness. Nor do I want to use my torch on the way to the yard in case it's seen.'

'It's going to be fun!' Dick whispered back. 'I hope Jock comes. It will be maddening if he doesn't.'

He did come. There was a scrambling over the heather and once again a shadow appeared at the tent opening.

'Julian! Dick! I've come. Are you ready?'

It was Jock's voice, of course. Dick's thumb pressed the switch of his torch and for a moment its light fell on Jock's red, excited face, and then was switched off again.

'Hallo, Jock! So you were able to come,' said Dick. 'I say, was that you in the lorry this morning, going by the Green Pool?'

'Yes. Did you see me? I saw you and waved like mad,' said Jock. 'I wanted to stop the lorry and get down and speak to you, but the driver's an awful bad-tempered sort of fellow. He wouldn't hear of stopping. Said my stepfather would be wild with him if he did. Did you see *him* – my stepfather, I mean? He was in his car behind.'

'Were you off to market or something?' asked Julian.

'I expect that's where the lorry was going,' said Jock. 'It was empty, so I suppose my stepfather was going to pick up something there. I came back in the car. The lorry was supposed to come later.'

'How did you like Cecil Dearlove?' asked Dick, grinning in the darkness.

'Awful! Worse than his name,' groaned Jock. 'Wanted me to play soldiers all the time! The frightful thing is I've got to have him at the farm for the day tomorrow. Another day wasted. What shall I do with him?'

'Roll him in the pig-sty,' suggested Dick. 'Or put him with Biddy's puppies and let him sleep there. Tell him to play soldiers with them.'

Jock chuckled. 'I wish I could. The worst of it is Mum is awfully pleased that my stepfather's got this Cecil boy for me to be friends with. Don't let's talk about it. Are you ready to start off?'

'Yes,' said Julian, and began to scramble quietly out of his bag. 'We didn't tell the girls. Anne doesn't want to come, and I don't want George to leave Anne by herself. Now, let's be very, very quiet till we're out of hearing.'

Dick got out of his bag too. The boys had not undressed that night, except for their coats, so all they had to do was to slip these on, and then crawl out of the tent.

'Which is the way – over there?' whispered

Jock. Julian took his arm and guided him. He hoped he wouldn't lose his way in the starlit darkness. The moorland look so different at night!

'If we make for that hill you can dimly see over there against the starlit sky, we should be going in the right direction,' said Julian. So on they went, keeping towards the dark hill that rose up to the west.

It seemed very much farther to the railway yard at night than in the daytime. The three boys stumbled along, sometimes almost falling as their feet caught in tufts of heather. They were glad when they found some sort of path they could keep on.

'This is about where we met the shepherd,' said Dick, in a low voice. He didn't know why he spoke so quietly. He just felt as if he must. 'I'm sure we can't be very far off now.'

They went on for some way, and then Julian pulled Dick by the arm. 'Look,' he said. 'Down there, I believe that's the old yard. You can see the lines gleaming faintly here and there.'

They stood on the heathery slope above the old yard, straining their eyes. Soon they could make out dim shapes. Yes, it was the railway yard all right.

Jock clutched Julian's sleeve. 'Look – there's a light down there! Do you see it?'

The boys looked – and sure enough, down in the yard towards the other side of it, was a small yellow light. They stared at it.

'Oh – I think I know what it is,' said Dick, at last. 'It's the light in the watchman's little hut – old Wooden-Leg Sam's candle. Don't you think so, Ju?'

'Yes. You're right,' said Julian. 'I tell you what we'll do – we'll creep right down into the yard, and go over to the hut. We'll peep inside and see if old Sam is there. Then we'll hide somewhere about and wait for the spook-train to come!'

They crept down the slope. Their eyes had got used to the starlight by now, and they were beginning to see fairly well. They got right down to the yard, where their feet made a noise on some cinders there.

They stopped. 'Someone will hear us if we make a row like this,' whispered Julian.

'Who will?' whispered back Dick. 'There's no one here except old Sam in his hut!'

'How do you know there isn't?' said Julian. 'Good heavens, Jock, don't make such a row with your feet!'

They stood there, debating what was the best thing to do. 'We'd better walk right round the edge of the yard,' said Julian at last. 'As far as I remember, the grass has grown there. We'll walk on that.'

So they made their way to the edge of the yard. Sure enough, there was grass there, and they walked on it without a sound. They went slowly and softly to where the light shone dimly in Sam's little hut.

The window was high and small. It was just about at the level of their heads, and the three boys cautiously eased themselves along to it and looked in.

Wooden-Leg Sam was there. He sat sprawled in a chair, smoking a pipe. He was reading a newspaper, squinting painfully as he did so. He obviously had not had his broken glasses mended yet. On a chair beside him was his wooden leg. He had unstrapped it, and there it lay.

'He's not expecting the spook-train tonight, or he wouldn't have taken off his wooden leg,' whispered Dick.

The candlelight flickered and shadows jumped about the tiny hut. It was a poor, ill-furnished little place, dirty and untidy. A cup without saucer or handle stood on the table, and a tin kettle boiled on a rusty stove.

Sam put down his paper and rubbed his eyes. He muttered something. The boys could not hear it, but they felt certain it was something about his broken glasses.

'Are there many lines in this yard?' whispered Jock, tired of looking in at old Sam. 'Where do they go to?'

'About half a mile or so up there is a tunnel,' said Julian, pointing past Jock. 'The lines come from there and run here, where they break up in many pairs – for shunting and so on, in the old days, I suppose, when this place was used.'

'Let's go up the lines to the tunnel,' said Jock. 'Come on. There's nothing to be seen here. Let's walk up to the tunnel.'

'All right,' said Julian. 'We may as well. I don't expect we'll see much up there either! I think these spook-trains are all a tall story of old Sam's!'

They left the little hut with its forlorn candle-light, and made their way round the yard again. Then they followed the single-track line away from the yard and up towards the tunnel. It didn't seem to matter walking on cinders now, and making a noise. They walked along, talk-ing in low voices.

And then things began to happen! A far-off muffled noise came rumbling out of the tunnel, which was now so near that the boys could see its black mouth. Julian heard it first. He stood still and clutched Dick.

'I say! Listen! Can you hear that?'

The others listened. 'Yes,' said Dick. 'But it's

only a train going through one of the underground tunnels – the noise is echoing out
through this one.'

'It isn't. That noise is made by a train coming
through this tunnel!' said Julian. The noise
grew louder and louder. A clanking made itself
heard too. The boys stepped off the lines and
crouched together by the side, waiting, hardly
daring to breathe.

Could it be the spook-train? They watched
for the light of an engine-lamp to appear like a
fiery eye in the tunnel. But none came. It was
darker than night in there! But the noise came
nearer and nearer and nearer. Could there be
the noise of a train without a train? Julian's
heart began to beat twice as fast, and Dick and
Jock found themselves clutching one another
without knowing it.

The noise grew thunderous, and then out
from the tunnel came something long and
black, with a dull glow in front that passed
quickly and was gone. The noise deafened the
boys, and then the clanking and rumbling grew

less as the train, or whatever it was, passed by. The ground trembled and then was still.

'Well, there you are,' said Julian, in a rather trembly voice. 'The spook-train – without a light or a signal! Where's it gone? To the yard, do you think?'

'Shall we go and see?' asked Dick. 'I didn't see anyone in the cab, even in the glow of what must have been the fire there – but there must be *someone* driving it! I say, what a weird thing, isn't it? It *sounded* real enough, anyway.'

'We'll go to the yard,' said Jock, who, of the three, seemed the least affected. 'Come on.'

They made their way very slowly – and then Dick gave a sharp cry. 'Blow! I've twisted my ankle. Half a minute!'

He sank down to the ground in great pain. It was only a sharp twist, not a sprain, but for a few minutes Dick could do nothing but groan. The others dared not leave him. Julian knelt by him, offering to rub the ankle, but Dick wouldn't let him touch it. Jock stood by anxiously.

It took about twenty minutes for Dick's ankle to be strong enough for him to stand on again. With the help of the others he got to his feet and tested his ankle. 'It's all right, I think. I can walk on it – slowly. Now we'll go to the yard and see what's happening!'

But even as they started to walk slowly back, they heard a noise coming up the lines from the far-away yard, 'Rumble, rumble, rumble, jangle, clank!'

'It's coming back again!' said Julian. 'Stand still. Watch! It'll be going back into the tunnel!'

They stood still and watched and listened. Again the noise came nearer and grew thunderous. They saw the glow of what might be the fire in the cab, and then it passed. The train disappeared into the blackness of the tunnel mouth and they heard the echo of its rumblings for some time.

'Well, there you are! There *is* a spook-train!' said Julian, trying to laugh, though he felt a good deal shaken. 'It came and it went – where from or where to, nobody knows! But we've heard it and seen it, in the darkness of the night. And jolly creepy it was, too!'

[11]
Mostly about Jock

The three boys stood rather close together, glad to feel each other in the darkness. They couldn't believe that they had found what they had come looking for so doubtfully! What kind of a train was this that had come rumbling out of the tunnel so mysteriously, and then, after a pause at the yard, had gone just as mysteriously back again?

'If only I hadn't twisted my ankle, we could have followed the train down the lines to the yard, and have gone quite close to it there,' groaned Dick. 'What an ass I am, messing things up at the most exciting moment!'

'You couldn't help it,' said Jock. 'I *say*! We've seen the spook-train! I can hardly believe it. Does it go all by itself, with nobody to drive it? Is it a real train?'

'Judging by the noise it made, it's real all right,' said Julian. 'And it shot out smoke, too. All the same, it's jolly strange. I can't say I like it much.'

'Let's go and see what's happened to Wooden-Leg Sam,' said Dick. 'I bet he's under his bed!'

They made their way slowly back to the yard, Dick limping a little, though his ankle was practically all right again. When they came to the yard they looked towards Sam's hut. The light was there no longer.

'He's blown it out and got under the bed!' said Dick. 'Poor Sam! It really must be terrifying for him. Let's go and peep into his hut.'

They went over to it and tried to see in at the window. But there was nothing to be seen. The hut was in complete darkness. Then suddenly a little flare flashed out somewhere near the floor.

'Look – there's Sam! He's lighting a match,' said Julian. 'See – he's peeping out from under the bed. He looks scared stiff. Let's tap on the window and ask him if he's all right.'

But that was quite the wrong thing to do! As soon as Julian tapped sharply on the window, Sam gave an anguished yell and retired hurriedly under the bed again, his wavering match-light going out.

'It's come for to take me!' they heard him wailing. 'It's come for to take me! And me with my wooden leg off too.'

'We're only frightening the poor old fellow,' said Dick. 'Come on. Let's leave him. He'll have a fit or something if we call out to him. He honestly thinks the spook-train's come to get him.'

They wandered round the dark yard for a few minutes, but there was nothing to find out in the darkness. No more rumbling came to their ears. The spook-train was evidently not going to run again that night.

'Let's go back,' said Julian. 'That really was exciting! Honestly, my hair stood on end when that train came puffing out of the tunnel. Where on earth did it come from? And what's the reason for it?'

They gave it up, and began to walk back to the camp. They scrambled through the heather, tired but excited. 'Shall we tell the girls we've seen the train?' said Dick.

'No,' said Julian. 'It would only scare Anne, and George would be furious if she knew we'd gone without her. We'll wait and see if we discover anything more before we say anything, either to the girls or to old Luffy.'

'Right,' said Dick. 'You'll hold your tongue, too, won't you, Jock?'

'Course,' said Jock, scornfully. 'Who would I tell? My stepfather? Not likely! How furious he'd be if he knew we'd all pooh-poohed his warnings and gone down to see the spook-train after all!'

He suddenly felt something warm against his legs, and gave a startled cry: 'What's this? Get away!'

But the warm thing turned out to be Timmy, who had come to meet three boys. He pressed against each of them in turn and whined a little.

'He says, "Why didn't you take me with you?"' said Dick. 'Sorry, old thing, but we couldn't. George would never have spoken to us again if we'd taken you, and left her behind! How would you have liked spook-trains, Timmy? Would you have run into a corner somewhere and hidden?'

'Woof,' said Timmy, scornfully. As if he would be afraid of anything!

They reached their camping-place and began to speak in whispers. 'Goodbye, Jock. Come up tomorrow if you can. Hope you don't have that Cecil boy to cope with!'

'Goodbye! See you soon,' whispered Jock, and disappeared into the darkness, with Timmy at his heels. Another chance of a midnight walk? Good, thought Timmy, just what he'd like! It was hot in the tent, and a scamper in the cool night air would be fine.

Timmy growled softly when they came near to Olly's Farm, and stood still, the hackles on his neck rising up a little. Jock put his hand on the dog's head and stopped.

'What's the matter, old boy? Burglars or something?'

He strained his eyes in the darkness. Big clouds now covered the stars and there was no light at all to see by. Jock made out a dim light in one of the barns. He crept over to it to see what it was. It went out as he came near, and then he heard the sound of footsteps, the quiet closing of the barn door, and the click of a padlock as it was locked.

Jock crept nearer – too near, for whoever it was must have heard him and swung round, lashing out with his arm. He caught Jock on the shoulder, and the boy overbalanced. He almost fell, and the man who had struck him clutched hold of him. A flash-light was put on and he blinked in the sudden light.

'It's you, Jock!' said an astonished voice, rough and impatient. 'What are you doing out here at this time of night?'

'Well, what are *you* doing?' demanded Jock, wriggling free. He switched on his own torch and let the light fall on the man who had caught him. It was Peters, one of the farm men, the one in whose lorry he had ridden that very day.

'What's it to do with you?' said Peters, angrily. 'I had a breakdown, and I've only just got back. Look here – you're fully dressed! Where have you been at this time of night? Did you hear me come in and get up to see what was happening?'

'You never know!' said Jock cheekily. He wasn't going to say anything that might make Peters suspicious of him. 'You just never know!'

'Is that Biddy?' said Peters, seeing a dark shadow slinking away. 'Do you mean to say you've been out with Biddy? What in the world have you been doing?'

Jock thanked his lucky stars that Peters hadn't spotted it was Timmy, not Biddy. He moved off without saying another word. Let Peters think what he liked! It was bad luck, though, that Peters had had a breakdown and come in late. If the man told his stepfather he'd seen Jock, fully dressed in the middle of the night, there'd be questions asked by both his mother and his stepfather, and Jock, who was a truthful boy, would find things very difficult to explain.

He scuttled off to bed, climbing up the pear-tree outside his window, and dropping quietly into his room. He opened his door softly to hear if anyone was awake in the house, but all was dark and silent.

'Blow Peters!' thought Jock. 'If he splits on me, I'm for it!'

He got into bed, pondered over the curious happenings of the night for a few minutes, and then slid into an uneasy sleep, in which spook-trains, Peters, and Timmy kept doing most peculiar things. He was glad to awake in the bright, sunny morning and find his mother shaking him.

'Get up, Jock! You're very late. Whatever's made you so sleepy? We're half-way through breakfast!'

Peters, apparently, didn't say anything to Jock's stepfather about seeing Jock in the night. Jock was very thankful. He began to plan how to slip off to the others at the camp. He'd take them some food! That would be a fine excuse.

'Mum, can I take a basket of stuff to the campers?' he said, after breakfast. 'They must be running short now.'

'Well, that boy is coming,' said his mother. 'What's his name – Cecil something? Your stepfather says he's such a nice boy. You did enjoy your day with him yesterday, didn't you?'

Jock would have said quite a lot of uncomplimentary things about dear Cecil if his stepfather had not been there, sitting by the window reading the paper. As it was, he shrugged his shoulders and made a face, hoping that his mother would understand his feelings. She did.

'What time is Cecil coming?' she said. 'Perhaps there's time for you to run to the camp with a basket.'

'I don't want him running off up there,' said Mr Andrews, suddenly butting into the conversation, and putting down his newspaper. 'Cecil may be here at any minute – and I know what Jock is! He'd start talking to those kids and forget all about coming back. Cecil's father is a great friend of mine, and Jock's got to be polite to him, and be here to welcome him. There's to be no running off to that camp today.'

Jock looked sulky. Why must his stepfather suddenly interfere in his plans like this? Rushing him off to the town, making him take Cecil for a friend! Just when some other children had come into his rather lonely life and livened it up, too! It was maddening.

'Perhaps I can go up to the camp myself with some food,' said his mother, comfortingly. 'Or maybe the children will come down for some.'

Jock was still sulky. He stalked out into the yard and went to look for Biddy. She was with her pups who were now trying to crawl round the shed after her. Jock hoped the campers would come to fetch food themselves that day. Then at least he would get a word with them.

Cecil arrived by car. He was about the same age as Jock, though he was small for twelve years old. He had curly hair which was too long, and his grey flannel suit was very, very clean and well-pressed.

'Hallo!' he called to Jock. 'I've come. What shall we play at? Soldiers?'

'No. Red Indians,' said Jock, who had suddenly remembered his old Red Indian head-dress with masses of feathers round it, and a trail of them falling down the back. He rushed indoors, grinning. He changed into the whole suit, and put on his head-dress. He took his paint-box and hurriedly painted a frightful pattern of red, blue and green on his face. He found his tomahawk and went downstairs. He would play at Red Indians, and scalp that annoying Pale-Face!

Cecil was wandering round by himself. To his enormous horror, as he turned a corner, a most terrifying figure rose up from behind a wall, gave a horrible yell and pounced on him, waving what looked like a dangerous chopper.

Cecil turned and fled, howling loudly, with Jock leaping madly after him, whooping for all he was worth, and thoroughly enjoying himself. He had had to play at soldiers all the day before with dear Cecil. He didn't see why Cecil shouldn't play Red Indians all day with him today!

Just at that moment, the four campers arrived to fetch food, with Timmy running beside them. They stopped in amazement at the sight of Cecil running like the wind, howling dismally, and a fully-dressed and painted Red Indian leaping fiercely after him.

Jock saw them, did a comical war-dance all round them, much to Timmy's amazement, yelled dramatically, pretended to cut off Timmy's tail and then tore after the vanishing Cecil.

The children began to laugh helplessly. 'Oh dear!' said Anne, with tears of laughter in her eyes, 'that must be Cecil he's after. I suppose this is Jock's revenge for having to play soldiers all day with him yesterday. Look, there they go round the pig-sty. Poor Cecil. He really thinks he's going to be scalped!'

Cecil disappeared into the farm kitchen, sobbing, and Mrs Andrews ran to comfort him. Jock made off back to the others, grinning all over his war-painted face.

'Hallo,' he said. 'I'm just having a nice quiet time with dear Cecil. I'm so glad to see you. I wanted to come over, but my stepfather said I wasn't to – I must play with Cecil. Isn't he frightful?'

'Awful,' everyone agreed.

'I say, will your mother be furious with you for frightening Cecil like that? Perhaps we'd better not ask her for any food yet?' said Julian.

'Yes, you'd better wait a bit,' said Jock, leading them to the sunny side of the haystack they had rested by before. 'Hallo, Timmy! Did you get back all right last night?'

Jock had completely forgotten that the girls didn't know of the happenings of the night before. Both Anne and George at once pricked up their ears. Julian frowned at Jock, and Dick gave him a secret nudge.

'What's up?' said George, seeing all this by-play. 'What happened last night?'

'Oh, I just came up to have a little night-talk

with the boys – and Timmy walked back with me,' said Jock, airily. 'Hope you didn't mind him coming, George.'

George flushed an angry red. 'You're keeping something from me,' she said to the boys. 'Yes, you are. I know you are. I believe you went off to the railway yard last night! Did you?'

There was an awkward silence. Julian shot an annoyed look at poor Jock, who could have kicked himself.

'Go on – tell me,' persisted George, an angry frown on her forehead. 'You beasts! You did go! And you never woke me up to go with you! Oh, I do think you're mean!'

'Did you see anything?' said Anne, her eyes going from one boy to another. Each of the girls sensed that there had been some kind of adventure in the night.

'Well,' began Julian. And then there was an interruption. Cecil came round the haystack, his eyes red with crying. He glared at Jock.

'Your father wants you,' he said. 'You're to

go at once. You're a beast, and I want to go home. Can't you hear your father yelling for you? He's got a stick – but I'm not sorry for you! I hope he whacks you hard!'

[12]

George loses her temper

Jock made a face at Cecil and got up. He went slowly off round the haystack, and the others listened in silence for whacks and yells. But none came.

'He frightened me,' said Cecil, sitting down by the others.

'Poor icle ting,' said Dick at once.

'Darling baby,' said George.

'Mother's pet,' said Julian. Cecil glared at them all. He got up again, very red.

'If I didn't know my manners, I'd smack your faces,' he said, and marched off hurriedly, before his own could be smacked.

The four sat in silence. They were sorry for Jock. George was angry and sulky because she knew the others had gone off without her the night before. Anne was worried.

They all sat there for about ten minutes. Then round the haystack came Jock's mother, looking distressed. She carried a big basket of food.

The children all stood up politely. 'Good-morning, Mrs Andrews,' said Julian.

'I'm sorry I can't ask you to stop today,' said Mrs Andrews. 'But Jock has really behaved very foolishly. I wouldn't let Mr Andrews give him a hiding because it would only make Jock hate his stepfather, and that would never do. So I've sent him up to bed for the day. You won't be able to see him, I'm afraid. Here is some food for you to take. Oh, dear – I'm really very sorry about all this. I can't think what came over Jock to behave in such a way. It's not a bit like him.'

Cecil's face appeared round the haystack, looking rather smug. Julian grinned to himself.

'Would you like us to take Cecil for a nice long walk over the moors?' he said. 'We can climb hills and jump over streams and scramble through the heather. It would make such a nice day for him.'

Cecil's face immediately disappeared.

'Well,' said Mrs Andrews, 'that really would be very kind of you. Now that Jock's been sent upstairs for the day there's no one for Cecil to play with. But I'm afraid he's a bit of a mother's boy, you know. You'll have to go carefully with him. Cecil! Cecil! Where are you? Come and make friends with these children.'

But Cecil had gone. There was no answer at all. He didn't want to make friends with 'these children'. He knew better than that! Mrs Andrews went in search of him, but he had completely disappeared.

The four children were not at all surprised. Julian, Dick and Anne grinned at one another. George stood with her back to them, still sulky.

Mrs Andrews came back again, out of breath. 'I can't find him,' she said. 'Never mind. I'll find something for him to do when he appears again.'

'Yes. Perhaps you've got some beads for him to thread? Or a nice easy jigsaw puzzle to do?' said Julian, very politely. The others giggled. A smile appeared on Mrs Andrews's face.

'Bad boy!' she said. 'Oh dear – poor Jock. Well it's his own fault. Now goodbye, I must get on with my work.'

She ran off to the dairy. The children looked round the haystack. Mr Andrews was getting into his car. He would soon be gone. They waited a few minutes till they heard the car set off down the rough cart-track.

'That's Jock's bedroom – where the pear-tree is,' said Julian. 'Let's just have a word with him before we go. It's a shame.'

They went across the farmyard and stood under the pear-tree – all except George, who stayed behind the haystack with the food, frowning. Julian called up to the window above: 'Jock!'

A head came out, the face still painted terrifyingly in streaks and circles. 'Hallo! He didn't whack me. Mum wouldn't let him. All the same, I'd rather he had – it's awful being stuck up here this sunny day. Where's dear Cecil?'

'I don't know. Probably in the darkest corner

of one of the barns,' said Julian. 'Jock, if things are difficult in the daytime, come up at night. We've got to see you somehow.'

'Right,' said Jock. 'How do I look? Like a real Red Indian?'

'You look frightful,' grinned Julian. 'I wonder old Timmy knew you.'

'Where's George?' asked Jock.

'Sulking behind the haystack,' said Dick. 'We shall have an awful day with her now. You let the cat properly out of the bag, you idjit!'

'Yes. I'm a ninny and an idjit,' said Jock, and Anne giggled. 'Look – there's Cecil. You might tell him to beware of the bull, will you?'

'Is there a bull?' said Anne, looking alarmed.

'No. But that's no reason why he shouldn't beware of one,' grinned Jock. 'So long! Have a nice day!'

The three left him, and strolled over to Cecil, who had just appeared out of a dark little shed. He made a face at them, and stood ready to run to the dairy where Mrs Andrews was busy.

Julian suddenly clutched Dick and pointed

behind Cecil. 'The bull! Beware of the bull!' he
yelled suddenly.

Dick entered into the joke. 'The bull's loose!
Look out! Beware of the bull!' he shouted.

Anne gave a shriek. It all sounded so real
that, although she knew it was a joke, she felt
half-scared. 'The bull!' she cried.

Cecil turned green. His legs shook. 'W-w-w-
where is it?' he stammered.

'Look out behind you!' yelled Julian, pointing. Poor Cecil, convinced that a large bull was
about to pounce on him from behind, gave an
anguished cry and tore on tottering legs to the
dairy. He threw himself against Mrs Andrews.

'Save me, save me! The bull's chasing me.'

'But there's no bull here,' said Mrs Andrews,
in surprise. 'Really, Cecil! Was it a pig after
you, or something?'

Helpless with laughter, the three children
made their way back to George. They tried
to tell her about the make-believe bull, but
she turned away and wouldn't listen. Julian
shrugged his shoulders. Best to leave George

to herself when she was in one of her rages! She didn't lose her temper as often as she used to, but when she did she was very trying indeed.

They went back to the camp with the basket of food. Timmy followed soberly. He knew something was wrong with George and he was unhappy. His tail was down, and he looked miserable. George wouldn't even pat him.

When they got back to the camp, George flared up.

'How dare you go off without me when I told you I meant to come? Fancy taking Jock and not letting me go! I think you're absolute beasts. I never really thought you'd do a thing like that, you and Dick.'

'Don't be silly, George,' said Julian. 'I told you we didn't mean to let you and Anne go. I'll tell you all that happened – and it's pretty thrilling!'

'What? Tell me quickly!' begged Anne, but George obstinately turned away her head as if she was not interested.

Julian began to relate all the curious happenings of the night. Anne listened breathlessly. George was listening too, though she pretended not to. She was very angry and very hurt.

'Well, there you are,' said Julian, when he had finished. 'If that's what people mean by spook-trains, there was one puffing in and out of that tunnel all right! I felt pretty scared, I can tell you. Sorry you weren't there too, George – but I didn't want to leave Anne alone.'

George was not accepting any apologies. She still looked furious.

'I suppose Timmy went with you,' she said. 'I think that was horrid of him – to go without waking me, when he knew I'd like to be with you on the adventure.'

'Oh, don't be so silly,' said Dick, in disgust. 'Fancy being angry with old Tim, too! You're making him miserable. And anyway, he *didn't* come with us. He just came to meet us when we got back, and then went off to keep Jock company on his way back to the farm.'

'Oh,' said George, and she reached out her

hand to pat Timmy, who was filled with de-light. 'At least Timmy was loyal to me then. That's something.'

There was a silence. Nobody ever knew quite how to treat George when she was in one of her moods. It was really best to leave her to herself, but they couldn't very well go off and leave the camp just because George was there, cross and sulky.

Anne took hold of George's arm. She was miserable when George behaved like this. 'George,' she began, 'there's no need to be cross with me, too. *I* haven't done anything!'

'If you weren't such a little coward, too afraid to go with us, I'd have been able to go too,' said George unkindly, dragging her arm away.

Julian was disgusted. He saw Anne's hurt face and was angry with George.

'Shut up, George,' he said. 'You're being horrid, saying catty things like that! I'm aston-ished at you.'

George was ashamed of herself, but she was too proud to say so. She glared at Julian.

'And *I'm* astonished at *you*,' she said. 'After all the adventures we've had together, you try to keep me out of this one. But you *will* let me come next time, won't you, Julian?'

'What! After your frightful behaviour to-day?' said Julian, who could be just as obstinate as George when he wanted to. 'Certainly not. This is my adventure and Dick's – and perhaps Jock's. Not yours or Anne's.'

He got up and stalked down the hill with Dick. George sat pulling bits of heather off the stems, looking mutinous and angry. Anne blinked back tears. She hated this sort of thing. She got up to get dinner ready. Perhaps after a good meal they would all feel better.

Mr Luffy was sitting outside his tent, reading. He had already seen the children that morning. He looked up, smiling.

'Hallo! Come to talk to me?'

'Yes,' said Julian, an idea uncurling itself in his mind. 'Could I have a look at that map of yours, Mr Luffy? The big one you've got showing every mile of these moorlands?'

'Of course. It's in the tent somewhere,' said Mr Luffy.

The boys found it and opened it. Dick at once guessed why Julian wanted it. Mr Luffy went on reading.

'It shows the railways that run under the moorlands too, doesn't it?' said Julian.

Mr Luffy nodded. 'Yes. There are quite a few lines. I suppose it was easier to tunnel under the moors from valley to valley rather than make a permanent way over the top of them. In any case, a railway over the moors would probably be completely snowed up in the winter-time.'

The boys bent their heads over the big map; it showed the railways as dotted lines when they went underground, but by long black lines when they appeared in the open air, in the various valleys.

They found exactly where they were. Then Julian's finger ran down the map a little and came to where a small line showed itself at the end of a dotted line.

He looked at Dick, who nodded. Yes – that showed where the tunnel was, out of which the spook-train had come, and the lines to the deserted yard. Julian's finger went back from the yard to the tunnel, where the dotted lines began. His finger traced the dotted lines a little way till they became whole lines again. That was where the train came out into another valley!

Then his finger showed where the tunnel that led from the yard appeared to join up with another one, that also ran for some distance before coming out into yet another valley. The boys looked at one another in silence.

Mr Luffy suddenly spotted a day-flying moth and got up to follow it. The boys took the chance of talking to one another.

'The spook-train either runs through its own tunnel to the valley beyond – or it turns off into this fork and runs along to the other valley,' said Julian, in a low voice. 'I tell you what we'll do, Dick. We'll get Mr Luffy to run us down to the nearest town to buy something – and we'll slip along to the station there and see if we can't make a few inquiries about these two tunnels. We may find out something.'

'Good idea,' said Dick, as Mr Luffy came back. 'I say, sir, are you very busy today? Could you possibly run us down to the nearest town after dinner?'

'Certainly, certainly,' said Mr Luffy, amiably. The boys looked at one another in delight. *Now* they might find out something! But they wouldn't take George with them. No – they would punish her for her bad temper by leaving her behind!

[13]

A thrilling plan

Anne called them to dinner. 'Come along!' she cried. 'I've got it all ready. Tell Mr Luffy there's plenty for him, too.'

Mr Luffy came along willingly. He thought Anne was a marvellous camp-housekeeper. He looked approvingly at the spread set out on a white cloth on the ground.

'Hm! Salad. Hard-boiled eggs. Slices of ham. And what's this – apple-pie! My goodness! Don't tell me you cooked that here, Anne.'

Anne laughed. 'No. All this came from the farm, of course. Except the lime juice and water.'

George ate with the others, but said hardly a word. She was brooding over her wrongs, and Mr Luffy looked at her several times, puzzled.

'Are you quite well, George?' he said, suddenly. George went red.

'Yes, thank you,' she said, and tried to be more herself, though she couldn't raise a smile at all. Mr Luffy watched her, and was relieved to see that she ate as much as the others. Probably had some sort of row, he guessed correctly. Well, it would blow over! He knew better than to interfere.

They finished lunch and drank all the lime juice. It was a hot day and they were very thirsty indeed. Timmy emptied all his dish of water and went and gazed longingly into the canvas bucket of washing-water. But he was too well-behaved to drink it, now that he knew he mustn't. Anne laughed, and poured some more water into his dish.

'Well,' said Mr Luffy, beginning to fill his old brown pipe, 'if anyone wants to come into town with me this afternoon, I'll be starting in fifteen minutes.'

'I'll come!' said Anne, at once. 'It won't take George and me long to wash up these things. Will you come too, George?'

'No,' said George, and the boys heaved a sigh

of relief. They had guessed she wouldn't want to come with them – but, if she'd known what they were going to try and find out, she would have come all right!

'I'm going for a walk with Timmy,' said George, when all the washing-up had been done.

'All right,' said Anne, who secretly thought that George would be much better left on her own to work off her ill-feelings that afternoon. 'See you later.'

George and Timmy set off. The others went with Mr Luffy to where his car was parked beside the great rock. They got in.

'Hi! The trailer's fastened to it,' called Julian. 'Wait a bit. Let me get out and undo it. We don't want to take an empty trailer bumping along behind us for miles.'

'Dear me. I always forget to undo the trailer,' said Mr Luffy, vexed. 'The times I take it along without meaning to!'

The children winked at one another. Dear old Luffy! He was always doing things like that.

No wonder his wife fussed round him like an old hen with one foolish chicken when he was at home.

They went off in the car, jolting over the rough road till they came to the smooth highway. They stopped in the centre of the town. Mr Luffy said he would meet them for tea at five o'clock at the hotel opposite the parking-place.

The three of them set off together, leaving Mr Luffy to go to the library and browse there. It seemed funny to be without George. Anne didn't much like it, and said so.

'Well, we don't like going off without George either,' said Julian. 'But honestly, she can't behave like that and get away with it. I thought she'd grown out of that sort of thing.'

'Well, you know how she adores an adventure,' said Anne. 'Oh dear – if I hadn't felt so scared you'd have taken me along, and George would have gone too. It's quite true what she said about me being a coward.'

'You're not,' said Dick. 'You can't help being

scared of things sometimes – after all, you're the youngest of us – but being scared doesn't make you a coward. I've known you to be as brave as any of us when you've been scared stiff!'

'Where are we going?' asked Anne. The boys told her, and her eyes sparkled.

'Oh – are we going to find out where the spook-train comes from? It might come from one of two valleys then, judging from the map.'

'Yes. The tunnels aren't really very long ones,' said Julian. 'Not more than a mile, I should think. We thought we'd make some inquiries at the station and see if there's anyone who knows anything about the old railway yard and the tunnel beyond. We shan't say a word about the spook-train of course.'

They walked into the station. They went up to a railway plan and studied it. It didn't tell them much. Julian turned to a young porter who was wheeling some luggage along.

'I say! Could you help us? We're camping up on the moorlands, and we're quite near a deserted railway yard with lines that run into an old tunnel. Why isn't the yard used any more?'

'Don't know,' said the boy. 'You should ask old Tucky there – see him? He knows all the tunnels under the moors like the back of his hand. Worked in them all when he was a boy.'

'Thanks,' said Dick, pleased. They went over to where an old whiskered porter was sitting in the sun, enjoying a rest till the next train came in.

'Excuse me,' said Julian politely. 'I've been told that you know all about the moorland tunnels like the back of your hand. They must be very, very interesting.'

'My father and my grandfather built those tunnels,' said the old porter, looking up at the children out of small faded eyes that watered in the strong sunlight. 'And I've been guard on all the trains that ran through them.'

He mumbled a long string of names, going through all the list of tunnels in his mind. The children waited patiently till he had finished.

'There's a tunnel near where we're camping

on the moorlands,' said Julian, getting a word in at last. 'We're not far from Olly's Farm. We came across an old deserted railway yard, with lines that led into a tunnel. Do you know it?'

'Oh yes, that's an old tunnel,' said Tucky, nodding his grey head, on which his porter's cap sat all crooked. 'Hasn't been used for many a long year. Nor the yard either. Wasn't enough traffic there, far as I remember. They shut up the yard. Tunnel isn't used any more.'

The boys exchanged glances. So it wasn't used any more! Well, they knew better.

'The tunnel joins another, doesn't it?' said Julian. The porter, pleased at their interest in the old tunnels he knew so well, got up and went into an office behind. He came out with a dirty, much-used map, which he spread out on his knee. His black finger-nail pointed to a mark on the map.

'That's the yard see? It was called Olly's Yard, after the farm. There're the lines to the tunnel. Here's the tunnel. It runs right through to Kilty Vale – there it is. And here's where it used to join the tunnel to Roker's Vale. But that was bricked up years ago. Something happened there – the roof fell in, I think it was – and the company decided not to use the tunnel to Roker's Vale at all.'

The children listened with the utmost interest. Julian reasoned things out in his mind. If that spook-train came from anywhere then it must come from Kilty Vale, because that was the only place the lines went to now, since the way to Roker's Vale had been bricked up where the tunnels joined.

'I suppose no trains run through the tunnel from Kilty Vale to Olly's Yard now, then?' he said.

Tucky snorted. 'Didn't I tell you it hasn't been used for years? The yard at Kilty Vale's been turned into something else, though the lines are still there. There's been no engine through that tunnel since I was a young man.'

This was all very, very interesting. Julian thanked old Tucky so profusely that he wanted to tell the children everything all over again. He even gave them the old map.

'Oh, thanks,' said Julian, delighted to have it. He looked at the others. 'This'll be jolly useful!' he said, and they nodded.

They left the pleased old man and went out into the town. They found a little park and sat down on a seat. They were longing to discuss all that Tucky had told them.

'It's jolly strange,' said Dick. 'No trains run there now – the tunnel's not been used for ages – and Olly's Yard must have been derelict for years.'

'And yet, there appear to be trains that come and go!' said Julian.

'Then, they *must* be spook-trains,' said Anne, her eyes wide and puzzled. 'Julian, they must be, mustn't they?'

'Looks like it,' said Julian. 'It's most mysterious. I can't understand it.'

'Ju,' said Dick, suddenly. 'I know what we'll do! We'll wait one night again till we see the spook-train come out of the tunnel to the yard. Then one of us can sprint off to the *other* end of the tunnel – it's only about a mile long – and

wait for it to come out the other side! Then
we'll find out why a train still runs from Kilty
Vale to Olly's Yard through that old tunnel.'

'Jolly good idea,' said Julian, thrilled. 'What
about tonight? If Jock comes, he can go, too. If
he doesn't, just you and I will go. *Not* George.'

They all felt excited. Anne wondered if she
would be brave enough to go too, but she knew
that when the night came she wouldn't feel half
as brave as she did now! No, she wouldn't go.
There was really no need for her to join in this
adventure at present. It hadn't even turned out
to be a proper one yet – it was only an unsolved
mystery!

George hadn't come back from her walk
when they reached the camp. They waited
for her, and at last she appeared with Timmy,
looking tired out.

'Sorry I was an ass this morning,' she said at
once. 'I've walked my temper off! Don't know
what came over me.'

'That's all right,' said Julian amiably. 'Forget
it.'

They were all very glad that George had recovered her temper, for she was a very prickly person indeed when she was angry. She was rather subdued and said nothing at all about spook-trains or tunnels. So they said nothing either.

The night was fine and clear. Stars shone out brilliantly again in the sky. The children said good-night to Mr Luffy at ten o'clock and got into their sleeping-bags. Julian and Dick did not mean to go exploring till midnight, so they lay and talked quietly.

About eleven o'clock they heard somebody moving cautiously outside. They wondered if it was Jock, but he did not call out to them. Who could it be?

Then Julian saw a familiar head outlined against the starlit sky. It was George. But what in the world was she doing? He couldn't make it out at all. Whatever it was she wasn't making any noise over it, and she obviously thought the boys were asleep. Julian gave a nice little snore or two just to let her go on thinking so.

At last she disappeared. Julian waited a few minutes and then put his head cautiously out of the tent opening. He felt about, and his fingers brushed against some string. He grinned to himself and got back into the tent.

'I've found out what George was doing,' he whispered. 'She's put string across the entrance of our tent, and I bet it runs to her tent and she's tied it to her big toe or something, so that if we go out without her she'll feel the pull of the string when we go through it and wake up and follow us!'

'Good old George,' chuckled Dick. 'Well, she'll be unlucky. We'll squeeze out under the sides of the tent!'

Which was what they did do at about a minute past twelve! They didn't disturb George's string at all. They were out on the heather and away down the slope while George was sleeping soundly in her tent beside Anne, waiting for the pull on her toe which didn't come. Poor George!

The boys arrived at the deserted railway yard

and looked to see if Wooden-Leg Sam's candle was alight. It was. So the spook-train hadn't come along *that* night, yet.

They were just scrambling down to the yard when they heard the train coming. There was the same rumbling noise as before, muffled by the tunnel – and then out of the tunnel, again with no lamps, came the spook-train, clanking on its way to the yard!

'Quick, Dick! You sprint off to the tunnel opening and watch for the train to go back in again. And I'll find my way across the moor to the other end of the tunnel. There was a path marked on that old map, and I'll follow that!' Julian's words tumbled over each other in his excitement. 'I'll jolly well watch for the spook-train to complete its journey, and see if it vanishes into thin air or what!'

And off he went to find the path that led over the moors to the other end of the tunnel. He meant to see what happened at the other end if he had to run all the way!

[14]

Jock comes to camp

Julian found the path quite by chance and went along it as fast as he could. He used his torch, for he did not think he would meet anyone out on such a lonely way at that time of night. The path was very much overgrown, but he could follow it fairly easily, even running at times.

'If that spook-train stops about twenty minutes in the yard again, as it did before, it will give me just about time to reach the other end of the tunnel,' panted Julian. 'I'll be at Kilty's Yard before it comes.'

It seemed a very long way. But at last the path led downwards, and some way below him Julian could see what might be a railway yard. Then he saw that big sheds were built there – or what looked like big sheds in the starlight.

He remembered what the old porter had

said. Kilty's Yard was used for something else now – maybe the lines had been taken up. Maybe even the tunnel had been stopped up, too. He slipped quickly down the path and came into what had once been the old railway yard. Big buildings loomed up on every side. Julian thought they must be workshops of some kind. He switched his torch on and off very quickly, but the short flash had shown him what he was looking for – two pairs of railway lines. They were old and rusty, but he knew they must lead to the tunnel.

He followed them closely, right up to the black mouth of the dark tunnel. He couldn't see inside at all. He switched his torch on and off quickly. Yes – the lines led right inside the tunnel. Julian stopped and wondered what to do.

'I'll sneak into the tunnel a little way and see if it's bricked up anywhere,' he thought. So in he went, walking between one pair of lines. He put on his torch, certain that no one would see its light and challenge him to say what he was doing out so late at night.

The tunnel stretched before him, a great yawning hole, disappearing into deep blackness. It was certainly not bricked up. Julian saw a little niche in the brickwork of the tunnel and decided to crouch in it. It was one of the niches made for workmen to stand in when trains went by in the old days.

Julian crouched down in the dirty old niche and waited. He glanced at the luminous face of his watch. He had been twenty minutes getting here. Maybe the train would be along in a few minutes. He would be very, very close to it! Julian couldn't help wishing that Dick was with him. It was so eerie waiting there in the dark for a mysterious train that apparently belonged to no one and came and went from nowhere to nowhere!

He waited and he waited. Once he thought he heard a rumble far away down the tunnel, and he held his breath, feeling certain that the train was coming. But it didn't come. Julian waited for half an hour and still the train had not appeared. What had happened to it?

'I'll wait another ten minutes and then I'm going,' Julian decided. 'I've had about enough of hiding in a dark, dirty tunnel waiting for a train that doesn't come! Maybe it has decided to stay in Olly's Yard for the night.'

After ten minutes he gave it up. He left the tunnel, went into Kilty's Yard and then up the path to the moors. He hurried along it, eager to see if Dick was at the other end of the tunnel. Surely he would wait there till Julian came back!

Dick was there, tired and impatient. When he saw a quick flash from Julian's torch he answered it with his own. The two boys joined company thankfully.

'You *have* been ages!' said Dick, reproachfully. 'What happened? The spook-train went back into the tunnel ages and ages ago. It only stayed about twenty minutes in the yard again.'

'Went back into the tunnel!' exclaimed Julian. 'Did it really? Well, it never came out the other side! I waited for ages. I never even heard it – though I did hear a very faint rumble once, or thought I did.'

The boys fell silent, puzzled and mystified. What sort of a train was this that puffed out of a tunnel at dead of night, and went back again, but didn't appear out of the other end?

'I suppose the entrance to that second tunnel the porter told us about *is* really bricked up?' said Julian at last. 'If it wasn't, the train could go down there, of course.'

'Yes. That's the only solution, if the train's a real one and not a spook one,' agreed Dick. 'Well, we can't go exploring the tunnels now – let's wait and do it in the daytime. I've had enough tonight!'

Julian had had enough too. In silence the two boys went back to camp. They quite forgot the string in front of their tent, and scrambled right through it. They got into the sleeping-bags thankfully.

The string, fastened to George's big toe through a hole she had cut in her sleeping-bag, pulled hard, and George woke up with a jump. Timmy was awake, having heard the boys come back. He licked George when she sat up.

George had not undressed properly. She slipped quickly out of her bag and crawled out of her tent. Now she would catch the two boys going off secretly and follow them!

But there was no sign or sound of them anywhere around. She crawled silently to their tent. Both boys had fallen asleep immediately, tired out with their midnight trip. Julian snored a little, and Dick breathed so deeply that George could quite well hear him as she crouched outside, listening. She was very puzzled. Someone had pulled at her toe – so somebody must have scrambled through that string. After listening for a few minutes, she gave it up and went back to her tent.

In the morning, George was furious! Julian and Dick related their night's adventure, and George could hardly believe that once again they had gone without her – and that they had managed to get away without disturbing the string! Dick saw George's face and couldn't help laughing.

'Sorry, old thing. We discovered your little trick and avoided it when we set out – but typically, we forgot all about it coming back. We must have given your toe a frightful tug. Did we? I suppose you *did* tie the other end of the string to your toe?'

George looked as if she could throw all the breakfast things at him. Fortunately for everyone Jock arrived at that moment. He didn't wear his usual beaming smile but seemed rather subdued.

'Hallo, Jock!' said Julian. 'Just in time for a spot of breakfast. Sit down and join us.'

'I can't,' said Jock. 'I've only a few minutes. Listen. Isn't it rotten – I'm to go away and stay with my stepfather's sister for two weeks! Two weeks! You'll be gone when I come back, won't you?'

'Yes. But, Jock, *why* have you got to go away?' said Dick, surprised. 'Has there been a row or something?'

'I don't know,' said Jock. 'Mum won't say, but she looks pretty miserable. My stepfather's in a frightful temper. It's my opinion they want me out of the way for some reason. I don't know this sister of my stepfather's very well – only met her once – but she's pretty awful.'

'Well, come over here and stay with us, if they want to get rid of you,' said Julian, sorry for Jock. Jock's face brightened.

'I *say*, that's a fine idea!' he said.

'Smashing,' agreed Dick. 'Well, I don't see what's to stop you. If they want to get rid of you, it can't matter where you go for a fortnight. We'd love to have you.'

'Right. I'll come,' said Jock. 'I'll not say a word about it, though, to my stepfather. I'll let Mum into the secret. She was going to take me away today, but I'll just tell her I'm coming to you instead. I don't think she'll split on me, and I hope she'll square things with my stepaunt.'

Jock's face beamed again now. The others beamed back, even George, and Timmy wagged his tail. It would be nice to have Jock – and what a lot they had to tell him.

He went off to break the news to his mother, while the others washed up and cleared things away. George became sulky again when Jock was gone. She simply could not or would not realise that Julian meant what he said!

When they began to discuss everything that had happened the night before, George refused to listen. 'I'm not going to bother about your stupid spook-trains any more,' she said. 'You wouldn't let me join you when I wanted to, and now I shan't take any interest in the matter.'

And she walked off with Timmy, not saying where she was going.

'Well, let her go,' said Julian, exasperated and cross. 'What does she expect me to do? Climb down and say we'll let her come the next night we go?'

'We said we'd go in the daytime,' said Dick. 'She could come then, because if Anne doesn't want to come it won't matter leaving her here alone in the daytime.'

'You're right,' said Julian. 'Let's call her back and tell her.' But by that time George was out of hearing.

'She's taken sandwiches,' said Anne. 'She means to be gone all day. Isn't she an idiot?'

Jock came back after a time, with two rugs and an extra jersey and more food. 'I had hard work to persuade Mum,' he said. 'But she said yes at last. Though mind you, I'd have come anyhow! I'm not going to be shoved about by my stepfather just out of spite. I *say* – isn't this great! I never thought I'd be camping out with you. If there isn't room in your tent for me, Julian, I can sleep out on the heather.'

'There'll be room,' said Julian. 'Hallo, Mr Luffy! You've been out early!'

Mr Luffy came up and glanced at Jock. 'Ah, is this your friend from the farm? How do you do? Come to spend a few days with us? I see you have an armful of rugs!'

'Yes. Jock's coming to camp a bit with us,' said Julian. 'Look at all the food he's brought. Enough to stand a siege!'

'It is indeed,' said Mr Luffy. 'Well, I'm going to go through some of my specimens this morning. What are you going to do?'

'Oh, mess about till lunch-time,' said Julian. 'Then we might go for a walk.'

Mr Luffy went back to his tent and they could hear him whistling softly as he set to work. Suddenly Jock sat up straight and looked alarmed.

'What's the matter?' asked Dick. Then he heard what Jock had heard. A shrill whistle blown loudly by somebody some way off.

'That's my stepfather's whistle,' said Jock. 'He's whistling for me. Mum must have told him, or else he's found out I've come over here.'

'Quick – let's scoot away and hide,' said Anne. 'If you're not here he can't take you back! Come on! Maybe he'll get tired of looking for you, and go.'

Nobody could think of a better idea, and certainly nobody wanted to face a furious Mr Andrews. All four shot down the slope and made their way to where the heather was high and thick. They burrowed into it and lay still, hidden by some high bracken.

Mr Andrews's voice could soon be heard, shouting for Jock, but no Jock appeared. Mr Andrews came out by Mr Luffy's tent. Mr Luffy, surprised at the shouting, put his head out of his tent to see what it was all about. He didn't like the look of Mr Andrews at all.

'Where's Jock?' Mr Andrews demanded, scowling at him.

'I really do not know,' said Mr Luffy.

'He's got to come back,' said Mr Andrews, roughly. 'I won't have him hanging about here with those kids.'

'What's wrong with them?' inquired Mr Luffy. 'I must say I find them very well-behaved and pleasant-mannered.'

Mr Andrews stared at Mr Luffy, and put him down as a silly, harmless old fellow who would probably help him to get Jock back if he went about it the right way.

'Now look here,' said Mr Andrews. 'I don't know who you are, but you must be a friend of the children's. And if so, then I'd better warn you they're running into danger. See?'

'Really? In what way?' asked Mr Luffy, mildly and disbelievingly.

'Well, there's bad and dangerous places about these moorlands,' said Mr Andrews. 'Very bad. I know them. And those children have been messing about in them. See? And if Jock comes here, he'll start messing about too, and I don't want him to get into any danger. It would break his mother's heart.'

'Quite,' said Mr Luffy.

'Well, will you talk to him and send him back?' said Mr Andrews. 'That railway yard now – that's a most dangerous place. And folks do say that there're spook-trains there. I wouldn't want Jock to be mixed up in anything of that sort.'

'Quite,' said Mr Luffy again, looking closely at Mr Andrews. 'You seem very concerned about this – er – railway yard.'

'Me? Oh, no,' said Mr Andrews. 'Never been near the horrible place. I wouldn't want to see spook-trains – make me run a mile! It's just that I don't want Jock to get into danger. I'd be most obliged if you'd talk to him and send him home, when they all come back from wherever they are.'

'Quite,' said Mr Luffy again, most irritatingly. Mr Andrews gazed at Mr Luffy's bland face and suddenly wished he could smack it. 'Quite, quite, quite!' Gr-r-r-r-r-r-r!

He turned and went away. When he had gone for some time, and was a small speck in the distance, Mr Luffy called loudly.

'He's gone! Please send Jock here so that I can – er – address a few words to him.'

Four children appeared from their heathery hiding-place. Jock went over to Mr Luffy, looking mutinous.

'I just wanted to say,' said Mr Luffy, 'that I quite understand why you want to be away from your stepfather, and that I consider it's no business of mine where you go in order to get away from him!'

Jock grinned. 'Oh, thanks awfully,' he said. 'I

thought you were going to send me back!' He rushed over to the others. 'It's all right,' he said. 'I'm going to stay, and, I say – what about going and exploring down that tunnel after lunch? We *might* find that spook-train then!'

'Good idea!' said Julian. 'We will! Poor old George – she'll miss that little adventure too!'

[15]

George has an adventure

George had gone off with one fixed idea in her mind. She was going to find out something about that mysterious tunnel! She thought she would walk over the moorlands to Kilty's Yard, and see what she could see there. Maybe she could walk right back through the tunnel itself!

She soon came to Olly's Yard. There it lay below her, with Wooden-Leg Sam pottering about. She went down to speak to him. He didn't see or hear her coming and jumped violently when she called to him.

He swung round, squinting at her fiercely. 'You clear off!' he shouted. 'I've been told to keep you children out of here, see? Do you want me to lose my job?'

'Who told you to keep us out?' asked George,

puzzled as to who could have known they had been in the yard.

'*He* did, see?' said the old man. He rubbed his eyes, and then peered at George short-sightedly again. 'I've broken my glasses,' he said.

'Who's "he" – the person who told you to keep us out?' said George.

But the old watchman seemed to have one of his sudden strange changes of temper again. He bent down and picked up a large cinder. He was about to fling it at George when Timmy gave a loud and menacing growl. Sam dropped his arm.

'You clear out,' he said. 'You don't want to get a poor old man like me into trouble, do you? You look a nice kind boy you do. You wouldn't get Wooden-Leg Sam into trouble, would you?'

George turned to go. She decided to take the path that led to the tunnel and peep inside. But when she got there there was nothing to see. She didn't feel that she wanted to walk all alone inside that dark mouth, so she took the path that Julian had taken the night before, over the top of the tunnel. But she left it half-way to look at a curious bump that jutted up from the heather just there.

She scraped away at the heather and found something hard beneath. She pulled at it but it would not give. Timmy, thinking she was obligingly digging for rabbits, came to help. He scrambled below the heather – and then he suddenly gave a bark of fright and disappeared!

George screamed: 'Timmy! What have you done? Where are you?'

To her enormous relief she heard Timmy's bark some way down. Where *could* he be? She called again, and once more Timmy barked.

George tugged at the tufts of heather, and then suddenly she saw what the curious mound was. It was a built-up vent-hole for the old tunnel – a place where the smoke came curling out in the days when trains ran there often. It had been barred across with iron, but the bars had rusted and fallen in, and heather had grown thickly over them.

'Oh, Timmy, you must have fallen down the vent,' said George, anxiously. 'But not very far down. Wait a bit and I'll see what I can do. If only the others were here to help!'

But they weren't, and George had to work all by herself to try and get down to the broken bars. It took her a very long time, but at last she had them exposed, and saw where Timmy had fallen down.

He kept giving short little barks, as if to say: 'It's all right. I can wait. I'm not hurt!'

George had to sit down and take a rest after her efforts. She was hungry, but she said to herself that she would *not* eat till she had somehow got down to Timmy, and found out where he was. Soon she began her task again.

She climbed down through the fallen-in vent. It was very difficult, and she was terrified of the rusty old iron bars breaking off under her weight. But they didn't.

Once down in the vent she discovered steps made of great iron nails projecting out. Some of them had thin rungs across. There had evidently once been a ladder up to the top of the vent. Most of the rungs had gone, but the iron nails that supported them still stood in the brick walls of the old round vent. She heard Timmy give a little bark. He was quite near her now.

Cautiously she went down the great hole. Her foot touched Timmy. He had fallen on a collection of broken iron bars, which, caught in part of the old iron ladder, stuck out from it, and made a rough landing-place for the dog to fall on.

'Oh, Timmy,' said George, horrified. 'However am I going to get you out of here? This hole goes right down into the tunnel.'

She couldn't possibly pull Timmy up the hole. It was equally impossible to get him down. He could never climb down the iron ladder, especially as it had so many rungs missing.

George was in despair. 'Oh, Timmy! Why did I lose my temper and walk out on the others to do some exploring all by myself? Don't fall, Timmy. You'll break your legs if you do.'

Timmy had no intention of falling. He was frightened, but so far his curious landing-place felt firm. He kept quite still.

'Listen, Tim,' said George, at last. 'The only thing I can think of is to climb down round it somehow and see how far it is to the tunnel itself. There might even be someone there to help! No, that's silly. There can't be. But I might find an old rope – anything – that I could use to help you down with. Oh, dear, what a horrible nightmare!'

George gave Timmy a reassuring pat, and then began to feel about for the iron rungs with her feet. Further down they were all there, and it was easy to climb lower and lower. She was soon down in the tunnel itself. She had her torch with her and switched it on. Then she nearly gave a scream of horror.

Just near to her was a silent train! She could

almost touch the engine. Was it – could it be – the spook-train itself? George stared at it, breathing fast.

It looked very, very old and out-of-date. It was smaller than the trains she was used to – the engine was smaller and so were the trucks. The funnel was longer and the wheels were different from those of ordinary trains. George stared at the silent train by the light of her torch, her mind in a muddle. She really didn't know *what* to think!

It *must* be the spook-train! It had come from this tunnel the night before, and had gone back again – and it hadn't run all the way through to Kilty's Yard, because Julian had watched for it, and it hadn't come out there. No – it had run here, to the middle of the dark tunnel, and there it stood, waiting for night so that it might run again.

George shivered. The train belonged to years and years ago! Who drove it at night? Did anybody? Or did it run along without a driver, remembering its old days and old ways? No,

that was silly. Trains didn't think or remember.
George shook herself and remembered Timmy.

And just at that very moment, poor Timmy
lost his foot-hold on the iron bars, and fell! He
had stretched out to listen for George, his foot
had slipped – and now he was hurtling down
the vent! He gave a mournful howl.

He struck against part of the ladder and that
stopped his headlong fall for a moment. But
down he went again, scrabbling as he fell,
trying to get hold of something to save himself.

George heard him howl and knew he was
falling. She was so horror-stricken that she
simply couldn't move. She stood there at the
bottom of the vent like a statue, not even
breathing.

Timmy fell with a thump beside her, and a
groan was jerked out of him. In a trice George
was down by him on her knees. 'Timmy! Are
you hurt? Are you alive? Oh, Timmy, say
something!'

'Woof,' said Timmy, and got up rather un-
steadily on his four legs. He had fallen on a pile

of the softest soot! The smoke of many, many years had sooted the walls of the vent, and the weather had sent it down to the bottom, until quite a pile had collected at one side. Timmy had fallen plump in the middle of it, and almost buried himself. He shook himself violently, and soot flew out all over George.

She didn't know or care. She hugged him, and her face and clothes grew as black as soot! She felt about and found the soft pile that had saved Timmy from being hurt.

'It's soot! I came down the other side of the vent, so I didn't know the soot was there. Oh, Timmy, what a bit of luck for you! I thought you'd be killed – or at least badly hurt,' said George.

He licked her sooty nose and didn't like the taste of it.

George stood up. She didn't like the idea of climbing up that horrid vent again – and, anyway, Timmy couldn't. The only thing to do was to walk out of the tunnel. She wouldn't have fancied walking through the tunnel before, in case she met the spook-train – but here it was, close beside her, and she had been so concerned about Timmy that she had quite forgotten it.

Timmy went over to the engine and smelt the wheels. Then he jumped up into the cab. Somehow the sight of Timmy doing that took away all George's fear. If Timmy could jump up into the spook-train, there couldn't be much for her to be afraid of!

She decided to examine the trucks. There were four of them, all covered trucks. Shining her torch, she climbed up into one of them, pulling Timmy up behind her. She expected to find it quite empty, unloaded many, many years ago by long-forgotten railwaymen.

But it was loaded with boxes! George was surprised. Why did a spook-train run about with boxes in it? She shone her torch on to one – and then quickly switched it out!

She had heard a noise in the tunnel. She crouched down in the truck, put her hand on Timmy's collar, and listened. Timmy listened, too, the hackles rising on his neck.

It was a clanging noise. Then there came a bang. Then a light shone out, and the tunnel was suddenly as bright as day!

The light came from a great lamp in the side of the tunnel. George peeped cautiously out through a crack in the truck. She saw that this place must be where the tunnel forked. One fork went on to Kilty's Yard – but surely the other fork was supposed to be bricked up? George followed the lines with her eyes. One set went on down the tunnel to Kilty's Yard, the other set ran straight into a great wall, which was built across the second tunnel, that once led to Roker's Yard.

'Yes – it *is* bricked up, just as the old porter told Julian,' said George to herself. And then she stared in the greatest amazement, clutching the side of the truck, hardly believing her eyes.

Part of the wall was opening before her! Before her very eyes, a great mass of it slid back in the centre of the wall – back and back – until a strange-shaped opening, about the size of the train itself, showed in the thick wall. George gasped. Whatever could be happening?

A man came through the opening. George felt sure she had seen him before somewhere. He came up to the engine of the train and swung himself into the cab.

There were all sorts of sounds then from the cab. What was the man doing? Starting the fire to run the train? George did not dare to try and see. She was trembling now, and Timmy pressed himself against her to comfort her.

Then came another set of noises – steam noises. The man must be going to start the engine moving. Smoke came from the funnel. More noises, and some clanks and clangs.

It suddenly occurred to George that the man might be going to take the train through that little opening in the bricked-up wall. Then – supposing he shut the wall up again – George would be a prisoner! She would be in the truck, hidden behind that wall, and the wall would be closed so that she couldn't escape.

'I must get out before it's too late,' thought George, in a panic. 'I only hope the man doesn't see me!'

But just as she was about to try and get out, the engine gave a loud 'choo-choo', and began to move backwards! It ran down the lines a little way, then forward again, and this time its wheels were on the set of lines that led to the second tunnel, where the small opening now showed so clearly in the wall.

George didn't dare to get out of the moving train. So there she crouched as the engine steamed quickly to the hole in the wall that stretched right across the other tunnel. That hole just fitted it! It must have been made for it, thought George, as the train moved through it.

The train went right through and came out in another tunnel. Here there was a bright light, too. George peered out through the crack. There was more than a tunnel here! What looked like vast caves stretched away on each side of the tunnel, and men lounged about in them. Who on earth were they, and what were they doing with that old train?

There was a curious noise at the back of the train. The hole in the stout brick wall closed up

once more! Now there was no way in or out.
'It's like the Open-Sesame trick in Ali Baba and
the Forty Thieves,' thought George. 'And, like
Ali Baba, I'm in the cave – and don't know the
way to get myself out! Thank goodness Timmy
is with me!'

The train was now at a standstill. Behind it
was the thick wall – and then George saw that
in front of it was a thick wall, too! This tunnel
must be bricked up in two places – and in
between was this extraordinary cavern, or
whatever it was. George puzzled her head over
the strange place, but couldn't make head or
tail of it.

'Well! Whatever would the others say if they
knew you and I were actually in the spook-train
itself, tucked away in its hiding-place where
nobody in the world can find it?' whispered
George to Timmy. 'What are we to do, Timmy?'

Timmy wagged his tail cautiously. He didn't
understand all this. He wanted to lie low for a
bit and see how things turned out.

'We'll wait till the men have gone away, Timmy,' whispered George. 'That is, if they ever do! Then we'll get out and see if we can manage that Open-Sesame entrance and get away. We'd better tell Mr Luffy about all this. There's something very strange and very mysterious here – and we've fallen headlong into it!'

[16]

In the tunnel again

Jock was really enjoying himself at the camp. He had a picnic lunch with the others, and ate as much as they did, looking very happy. Mr Luffy joined them, and Jock beamed at him, feeling that he was a real friend.

'Where's George?' asked Mr Luffy.

'Gone off by herself,' said Julian.

'Have you quarrelled, by any chance?' said Mr Luffy.

'A bit,' said Julian. 'We have to let George get over it by herself, Mr Luffy. She's like that.'

'Where's she gone?' said Mr Luffy, helping himself to a tomato. 'Why isn't she back to dinner?'

'She's taken hers with her,' said Anne. 'I feel a bit worried about her, somehow. I hope she's all right.'

Mr Luffy looked alarmed. 'I feel a bit worried myself,' he said. 'Still, she's got Timmy with her.'

'We're going off on a bit of exploring,' said Julian, when they had all finished eating. 'What are *you* going to do, Mr Luffy?'

'I think I'll come with you,' said Mr Luffy, unexpectedly. The children's hearts sank. They couldn't possibly go exploring for spook-trains in the tunnel if Mr Luffy was with them.

'Well – I don't think it will be very interesting for you, sir,' said Julian, rather feebly. However, Mr Luffy took the hint and realised he wasn't wanted that afternoon.

'Right,' he said. 'In that case I'll stay here and mess about.'

The children sighed with relief. Anne cleared up, with Jock helping her, and then they called goodbye to Mr Luffy and set off, taking their tea with them.

Jock was full of excitement. He was so pleased to be with the others, and he kept thinking of sleeping in the camp that night –

what fun it would be! Good old Mr Luffy, taking his side like that. He bounded after the others joyfully as they went off to the old railway yard.

Wooden-Leg Sam was pottering about there as usual. They waved to him, but he didn't wave back. Instead he shook his fist at them and tried to bawl in his husky voice: 'You clear out! Trespassing, that's what you are. Don't you come down here or I'll chase you!'

'Well, we won't go down then,' said Dick, with a grin. 'Poor old man – thinking of chasing us with that wooden leg of his. We won't give him the chance. We'll just walk along here, climb down the lines and walk up them to the tunnel.'

Which is what they did, much to the rage of poor Sam. He yelled till his voice gave out, but they took no notice, and walked quickly up the lines. The mouth of the tunnel looked very round and black as they came near.

'Now we'll jolly well walk right through this tunnel and see where that spook-train is that came out of it the other night,' said Julian. 'It didn't come out the other end, so it *must* be somewhere in the middle of the tunnel.'

'If it's a real spook-train, it might completely disappear,' said Anne, not liking the look of the dark tunnel at all. The others laughed.

'It won't have disappeared,' said Dick. 'We shall come across it somewhere, and we'll examine it thoroughly and try and find out exactly what it is, and why it comes and goes in such a mysterious manner.'

They walked into the black tunnel, and switched on their torches, which made little gleaming paths in front of them. They walked up the middle of one pair of lines, Julian in front keeping a sharp look-out for anything in the shape of a train!

The lines ran on and on. The children's voices sounded weird and echoing in the long tunnel. Anne kept close to Dick, and half wished she hadn't come. Then she remembered that George had called her a coward, and she put up her head, determined not to show that she was scared.

Jock talked almost without stopping. 'I've never done anything like this in my life. I call this a proper adventure, hunting for spook-trains in a dark tunnel. It makes me feel nice and shivery all over. I do hope we find the train. It simply *must* be here somewhere!'

They walked on and on and on. But there was no sign of any train. They came to where the tunnel forked into the second one, that used to run to Roker's Vale. Julian flashed his torch on the enormous brick wall that stretched across the second tunnel.

'Yes, it's well and truly bricked up,' he said. 'So that only leaves this tunnel to explore. Come on.'

They went on again, little knowing that George and Timmy were behind that brick wall, hidden in a truck of the spook-train itself! They walked on and on down the lines, and found nothing interesting at all.

They saw a little round circle of bright light some way in front of them. 'See that?' said Julian. 'That must be the end of this tunnel –

the opening that goes into Kilty's Yard. Well, if the train isn't between here and Kilty's Yard, it's gone!'

In silence they walked down the rest of the tunnel, and came out into the open air. Workshops were built all over Kilty's Yard. The entrance to the tunnel was weed-grown and neglected. Weeds grew even across the lines there.

'Well, no train has been out of this tunnel here for years,' said Julian, looking at the thick weeds. 'The wheels would have chopped the weeds to bits.'

'It's extraordinary,' said Dick, puzzled. 'We've been right through the tunnel and there's no train there at all, yet we know it goes in and out of it. What's happened to it?'

'It *is* a spook-train,' said Jock, his face red with excitement. 'Must be. It only exists at night, and then comes out on its lines, like it used to do years ago.'

'I don't like thinking that,' said Anne, troubled. 'It's a horrid thought.'

'What are we going to do now?' Julian asked. 'We seem to have come to a blank. No train, nothing to see, empty tunnel. What a dull end to an adventure.'

'Let's walk back all the way again,' said Jock – he wanted to squeeze as much out of this adventure as he could. 'I know we shan't see the train this time any more than we did the last time, but you never know!'

'I'm not coming through that tunnel again,' said Anne. 'I want to be out in the sun. I'll walk over the top of the tunnel, along the path there that Julian took the other night and you three can walk back, and meet me at the other end.'

'Right,' said Julian and the three boys disappeared into the dark tunnel. Anne ran up the path that led alongside the top of it. How good it was to be in the open air again! That horrid tunnel! She ran along cheerfully, glad to be out in the sun.

She got to the other end of the tunnel quite quickly, and sat down on the path above the yard to wait for the others. She looked for

Wooden-Leg Sam. He was nowhere to be seen.
Perhaps he was in his little hut.

She hadn't been there for more than two
minutes when something surprising happened.
A car came bumping slowly down the rough
track to the yard! Anne sat up and watched. A
man got out – and Anne's eyes almost fell out of
her head. Why, it was – surely it was
Mr Andrews, Jock's stepfather!

He went over to Sam's hut and threw open
the door. Anne could hear the sound of voices.
Then she heard another noise – the sound of a
heavy lorry coming. She saw it come cautiously
down the steep, rough track. It ran into an old
tumbledown shed and stayed there. Then three
men came out and Anne stared at them. Where
had she seen them before?

'Of course! They're the farm labourers at
Jock's farm!' she thought. 'But what are they
doing here? How very strange!'

Mr Andrews joined the men and, to Anne's
dismay, they began to walk up the lines to the
tunnel! Her heart almost stopped. Goodness,

Julian, Dick and Jock were still in that tunnel, walking through it. They would bump right into Mr Andrews and his men – and then what would happen? Mr Andrews had warned them against going there, and had ordered Jock not to go.

Anne stared at the four men walking into the far-off mouth of the tunnel. What could she do? How could she warn the boys? She couldn't! She would just have to stay there and wait for them to come out – probably chased by a furious Mr Andrews and the other men. Oh dear, dear – if they were caught they would probably all get an awful telling off! What *could* she do?

'I can only wait,' thought poor Anne. 'There's nothing else to do. Oh, do come, Julian, Dick and Jock. I daren't do anything but wait for you.'

She waited and waited. It was now long past tea-time. Julian had the tea, so there was nothing for Anne to eat. Nobody came out of the tunnel. Not a sound was heard. Anne at last

decided to go down and ask Wooden-Leg Sam
a few questions. So, rather afraid, the girl set off
down to the yard.

Sam was in his hut, drinking cocoa, and
looking very sour. Something had evidently
gone wrong. When he saw Anne's shadow
across the doorway he got up at once, shaking
his fist.

'What, you children again! You went into
that tunnel this afternoon, and so I went up and
telephoned Mr Andrews to come and catch you
all, poking your noses in all the time? How did
you get out of that tunnel? Are the others with
you? Didn't Mr Andrews catch you, eh?'

Anne listened to all this in horror. So old Sam
had actually managed to telephone
Mr Andrews, and tell tales on them – so that
Jock's stepfather and his men had come to
catch them. This was worse than ever.

'You come in here,' said Sam suddenly, and
he darted his big arm at her. 'Come on. I don't
know where the others are, but I'll get one of
you!'

Anne gave a scream and ran away at top speed. Wooden-Leg Sam went after her for a few yards and then gave it up. He bent down and picked up a handful of cinders. A shower of them fell all round Anne, and made her run faster than ever.

She tore up the path to the heather, and was soon on the moors again, panting and sobbing. 'Oh, Julian! Oh, Dick! What's happened to you? Oh, where's George? If only she would come home, she'd be brave enough to look for them, but I'm not. I must tell Mr Luffy. He'll know what to do!'

She ran on and on, her feet catching continually in the tufts of thick heather. She kept falling over and scrambling up again. She now had only one idea in her mind – to find Mr Luffy and tell him every single thing! Yes, she would tell him about the spook-trains and all. There was something strange and important about the whole thing now, and she wanted a grown-up's help.

She staggered on and on. 'Mr Luffy! Oh, Mr Luffy, where are you? MR LUFFY!'

But no Mr Luffy answered her. She came round the gorse bushes she thought were the ones sheltering the camp – but, alas, the camp was not there. Anne had lost her way!

'I'm lost,' said Anne, the tears running down her cheeks. 'But I mustn't get scared. I must try to find the right path now. Oh, dear, I'm quite lost! Mr LUFFY!'

Poor Anne. She stumbled on blindly, hoping to come to the camp, calling every now and again. 'Mr Luffy. Can you hear me? MR LUFFFFFFFY!'

[17]

An amazing find

In the meantime, what had happened to the three boys walking back through the tunnel? They had gone slowly along examining the lines to see if a train could have possibly run along them recently. Few weeds grew in the dark airless tunnel, so they could not tell by those.

But, when they came about half-way, Julian noticed an interesting thing. 'Look,' he said, flashing his torch on to the lines before and behind them. 'See that? The lines are black and rusty behind us now, but here this pair of lines is quite bright – as if they had been used a lot.'

He was right. Behind them stretched black and rusty lines, sometimes buckled in places – but in front of them, stretching to the mouth of the tunnel leading to Olly's Yard, the lines were bright, as if train-wheels had run along them.

'That's funny,' said Dick. 'Looks as if the spook-train ran only from here to Olly's Yard and back. But why? And where in the world is it now? It's vanished into thin air!'

Julian was as puzzled as Dick. Where *could* a train be if it was not in the tunnel? It had obviously run to the middle of the tunnel, and then stopped – but where had it gone now?

'Let's go to the mouth of the tunnel and see if the lines are bright all the way,' said Julian at last. 'We can't discover much here – unless the train suddenly materialises in front of us!'

They went on down the tunnel, their torches flashing on the lines in front of them. They talked earnestly as they went. They didn't see four men waiting for them, four men who crouched in a little niche at the side of the tunnel, waiting there in the dark.

'Well,' said Julian, 'I think—' and then he stopped, because four dark figures suddenly pounced on the three boys and held them fast.

Julian gave a shout and struggled, but the man who had hold of him was far too strong to escape from. Their torches were flung to the ground. Julian's broke, and the other two torches lay there, their beams shining on the feet of the struggling company.

It didn't take more than twenty seconds to make each boy a captive, his arms behind his back. Julian tried to kick, but his captor twisted his arm so fiercely that he groaned in pain and stopped his kicking.

'Look here! What's all this about?' demanded Dick. 'Who are you, and what do you think you're doing? We're only three boys exploring an old tunnel. What's the harm in that?'

'Take them all away,' said a voice that everyone recognised at once.

'Mr Andrews! Is it you?' cried Julian. 'Set us free. You know us – the boys at the camp. And Jock's here too. What do you think you're doing?'

Mr Andrews didn't answer, but he gave poor

Jock a box on the right ear that almost sent him to the ground.

Their captors turned them about, and led them roughly up the tunnel, towards the middle. Nobody had a torch so it was all done in the darkness and the three boys stumbled badly, though the men seemed sure-footed enough.

They came to a halt after a time. Mr Andrews left them and Julian heard him go off somewhere to the left. Then there came a curious noise – a bang, a clank, and then a sliding, grating sound. What could be happening? Julian strained his eyes in the darkness, but he could see nothing at all.

He didn't know that Mr Andrews was opening the bricked-up wall through which the train had gone. He didn't know that he and the others were being pushed out of the first tunnel into the other one, through the curious hole in the wall. The three boys were shoved along in the darkness, not daring to protest.

Now they were in the curious place between the two walls which were built right across the place where the second tunnel forked from the first one. The place where the spook-train stood in silence – the place where George was, still hidden in one of the trucks with Timmy! But nobody knew that, of course; not even Mr Andrews guessed that a girl and a dog were listening in a truck nearby!

He put on a torch and flashed it in the faces of the three boys, who, although they were not showing any fear, felt rather scared all the same. This was so weird and unexpected, and they had no idea where they were at all.

'You were warned not to go down to that yard,' said the voice of one of the men. 'You were told it was a bad and dangerous place. So it is. And you've got to suffer for not taking heed of the warning! You'll be tied up and left here till we've finished our business. Maybe that'll be three days, maybe it'll be three weeks!'

'Look here, you can't keep us prisoner for all that time!' said Julian, alarmed. 'Why, there will be search parties out for us all over the place! They will be sure to find us.'

'Oh, no they won't,' said the voice. 'Nobody will find you here. Now, Peters – tie 'em up!'

Peters tied the three boys up. They had their legs tied, and their arms too, and were set down roughly against a wall. Julian protested again.

'What are you doing this for? We're quite harmless. We don't know a thing about your business, whatever it is.'

'We're not taking any chances,' said the voice. It was not Mr Andrews's voice, but a firm, strong one, full of determination and a large amount of annoyance.

'What about Mum?' said Jock suddenly, to his stepfather. 'She'll be worried.'

'Well, let her be worried,' said the voice again, answering before Mr Andrews could say a word. 'It's your own fault. You were warned.'

The feet of the four men moved away. Then there came the same noises again as the boys had heard before. They were made by the hole in the wall closing up, but the boys didn't know that. They couldn't imagine what they were.

The noises stopped and there was dead silence. There was also pitch darkness. The three boys strained their ears, and felt sure that the men had gone.

'Well! The brutes! Whatever are they up to?' said Julian in a low voice, trying to loosen the ropes round his hands.

'They've got some secret to hide,' said Dick. 'Gosh, they've tied my feet so tightly that the rope is cutting into my flesh.'

'What's going to happen?' came Jock's scared voice. This adventure didn't seem quite so grand to him now.

'Sh!' said Julian suddenly. 'I can hear something!'

They all lay and listened. What was it they could hear?

'It's – it's a dog whining,' said Dick, suddenly.

It was. It was Timmy in the truck with George. He had heard the voices of the boys he knew, and he wanted to get to them. But George, not sure yet that the men had gone, still had her hand on his collar. Her heart beat for joy to think she was alone no longer. The three boys – and Anne, too, perhaps – were there, in the same strange place as she and Timmy were.

The boys listened hard. The whining came again. Then, George let go her hold of Timmy's collar, and he leapt headlong out of the truck. His feet pattered eagerly over the ground. He went straight to the boys in the darkness, and Julian felt a wet tongue licking his face. A warm body pressed against him, and a little bark told him who it was.

'Timmy! I say, Dick – it's Timmy!' cried Julian, in joy. 'Where did he come from? Timmy, is it really you?'

'Woof,' said Timmy, and licked Dick next and then Jock.

'Where's George then?' wondered Dick.

'Here,' said a voice, and out of the truck scrambled George, switching on her torch as she did so. She went over to the boys. 'Whatever's happened? How did you come here? Were you captured or something?'

'Yes,' said Julian. 'But, George – where are we? And what are *you* doing here too? It's like a peculiar dream!'

'I'll cut your ropes first, before I stop to explain anything,' said George, and she took out her sharp knife. In a few moments she had cut the boys' bonds, and they all sat up, rubbing their sore ankles and wrists, groaning.

'Thanks, George! Now I feel fine,' said Julian, getting up. 'Where *are* we? Gracious, is that an engine there? What's it doing here?'

'That, Julian, is the spook-train!' said George, with a laugh. 'Yes, it is, really.'

'But we walked all the way down the tunnel and out of the other end, without finding it,' said Julian puzzled. 'It's most mysterious.'

'Listen, Ju,' said George. 'You know where that second tunnel is bricked up, don't you? Well, there's a way in through the wall – a whole bit of it moves back in a sort of Open-Sesame manner! The spook-train can run in through the hole, on the rails. Once it's beyond the wall it stops, and the hole is closed up again.'

George switched her torch round to show the astonished boys the wall through which they had come. Then she swung her torch to the big wall opposite. 'See that?' she said. 'There are *two* walls across this second tunnel, with a big space in between – where the spook-train hides! Clever, isn't it?'

'It would be, if I could see any sense in it,' said Julian. 'But I can't. Why should anyone mess about with a silly spook-train at night?'

'That's what we've got to find out,' said George. 'And now's our chance. Look, Julian – look at all the caves stretching out on either side of the tunnel here. They would make wonderful hiding-places!'

'What for?' said Dick. 'I can't make head or tail of this!'

George swung her torch on the three boys and then asked a sudden question: 'I say – where's Anne?'

'Anne! She didn't want to come back with us through the tunnel, so she ran over the moorlands to meet us at the other end, by Olly's

Yard,' said Julian. 'She'll be worried stiff, won't she, when we don't turn up? I only hope she doesn't come wandering up the tunnel to meet us – she'll run into those men if she does.'

Everyone felt worried. Anne hated the tunnel and she would be very frightened if people pounced on her in the darkness. Julian turned to George.

'Swing your torch round and let's see these caves. There doesn't seem to be anyone here now. We could have a snoop round.'

George swung her torch round, and Julian saw vast and apparently fathomless caves stretching out on either side, cut out of the sides of the tunnel. Jock saw something else. By the light of the torch he caught sight of a switch on the wall. Perhaps it opened the hole in the wall.

He crossed to it and pulled it down. Immediately the place was flooded with a bright light. It was a light-switch he had found. They all blinked in the sudden glare.

'That's better,' said Julian, pleased. 'Good

for you, Jock! Now we can see what we're doing.'

He looked at the spook-train standing silently near them on its rails. It certainly looked very old and forgotten – as if it belonged to the last century, not to this.

'It's quite a museum piece,' said Julian, with interest. 'So that's what we heard puffing in and out of the tunnel at night – old Spooky!'

'I hid in that truck there,' said George, pointing, and she told them her own adventure. The boys could hardly believe she had actually puffed into this secret place, hidden on the spook-train itself!

'Come on – now let's look at these caves,' said Dick. They went over to the nearest one. It was packed with crates and boxes of all kinds. Julian pulled one open and whistled.

'All black market stuff, I imagine. Look here – crates of tea, crates of whisky and brandy, boxes and boxes of stuff – goodness knows what! This is a real black market hiding-place!'

The boys explored a little further. The caves

were piled high with valuable stuff, worth
thousands of pounds.

'All stolen, I suppose,' said Dick. 'But what
do they *do* with it? I mean – how do they
dispose of it? They bring it here in the train,
of course, and hide it – but they must have some
way of getting rid of it.'

'Would they repack it on the train and run it
back to the yard when they had enough lorries
to take it away?' said Julian.

'No!' said Dick. 'Of course not. Let me see –
they steal it, pile it on to lorries at night, take it
somewhere temporarily . . .'

'Yes – to my mother's farm!' said Jock, in a
scared voice. 'All those lorries there in the barn
– that's what they're used for! And they come
down to Olly's Yard at night and the stuff is
loaded in secret on the old train that comes
puffing out to meet them – and then it's taken
back here and hidden!'

'Wheeeee-ew!' Julian whistled. 'You're right,
Jock! That's just what happens. What a cun-
ning plot – to use a perfectly honest little farm

as a hiding-place, to stock the farm with black-market men for labourers – no wonder they are such bad workers – and to wait for dark nights to run the stuff down to the yard and load it on the train!'

'Your stepfather must make a lot of money at this game,' said Dick to Jock.

'Yes. That's why he can afford to pour money into the farm,' said Jock, miserably. 'Poor Mum. This will break her heart. All the same, I don't think my stepfather's the chief one in this. There's somebody behind him.'

'Yes,' said Julian, thinking of the mean little Mr Andrews, with his big nose and weak chin. 'There probably is. Now – I've thought of something else. If this stuff is got rid of in any other way except down the tunnel it came up, there must somewhere be a way out of these caves!'

'I believe you're right,' said George. 'And if there is – we'll find it! And what's more, we'll escape that way!'

'Come on!' said Julian, and he switched off the glaring light. 'Your torch will give enough light now. We'll try this cave first. Keep your eyes open, all of you!'

[18]

A way of escape

The four children and Timmy went into the big cave. They made their way round piles of boxes, chests and crates, marvelling at the amount the men must have stolen from time to time.

'These aren't man-made caves,' said Julian. 'They're natural. I expect the roof did perhaps fall in where the two tunnels met, and the entrance between them was actually blocked up.'

'But were *two* walls built then?' said Dick.

'Oh, no. We can't guess how it was that this black market hiding-place came into existence,' said Julian, 'but it might perhaps have been known there were caves here – and when someone came prospecting along the tunnel one day, maybe they even found an old train buried under a roof-fall or something like that.'

'And resurrected it, and built another wall secretly for a hiding-place – and used the train for their own purposes!' said Dick. 'Made that secret entrance, too. How ingenious!'

'Or it's possible the place was built during the last war,' said Julian. 'Maybe secret experiments were carried on here – and given up afterwards. The place might have been discovered by the black marketeers then, and used in this clever way. We can't tell!'

They had wandered for a good way in the cave by now, without finding anything of interest beyond the boxes and chests of all kinds of goods. Then they came to where a pile was very neatly arranged, with numbers chalked on boxes that were built up one on top of another. Julian halted.

'Now this looks as if these boxes were about to be shifted off somewhere,' he said. 'All put in order and numbered. Surely the exit must be somewhere here?'

He took George's torch from her and flashed it all round. Then he found what he wanted.

The beam of light shone steadily on a strong roughly-made wooden door, set in the wall of the cave. They went over to it in excitement.

'This is what we want!' said Julian. 'I bet this is the exit to some very lonely part of the moors, not far from a road that lorries can come along to collect any goods carried out of here! There are some very deserted roads over these moors, running in the middle of miles of lonely moorland.'

'It's a clever organisation,' said Dick. 'Lorries stored at an innocent farm, full of goods for hiding in the tunnel-caves at a convenient time. The train comes out in the dark to collect the goods, and takes them back here, till the hue and cry after the goods has died down. Then out they go through this door to the moorlands, down to the lorries which come to collect them and whisk them away to the black market!'

'I told you how I saw Peters late one night, locking up the barn, didn't I?' said Jock, excitedly. 'Well, he must have got the lorry full of stolen goods then – and the next night he loaded them on to the spook-train!'

'That's about it,' said Julian, who had been trying the door to see if he could open it. 'I say, this door's maddening. I can't make it budge an inch. There's no lock that I can see.'

They all shoved hard, but the door would not give at all. It was very stout and strong, though rough and unfinished. Panting and hot, the four of them at last gave it up.

'Do you know what I think?' said Dick. 'I think the beastly thing has got something jammed hard against it on the outside.'

'Sure to have, when you come to think of it,' said Julian. 'It will be well hidden too – heather and bracken and stuff all over it. Nobody would ever find it. I suppose the lorry-drivers come across from the road to open the door when they want to collect the goods. And shut it and jam it after them.'

'No way of escape there, then,' said George in disappointment.

''Fraid not,' said Julian. George gave a sigh.

'Tired, old thing?' Julian asked kindly. 'Or hungry?'

'Both,' said George.

'Well, we've got some food somewhere, haven't we?' said Julian. 'I remember one of the men slinging my bag in after me. We've not had what we brought for tea yet. What about having a meal now? We can't seem to escape at the moment.'

'Let's have it here,' said George. 'I simply can't go a step further!'

They sat down against a big crate. Dick undid his kit-bag. There were sandwiches, cake and chocolate. The four of them ate thankfully, and wished they had something to wash down the food with. Julian kept wondering about Anne.

'I wonder what she did,' he said. 'She'd wait and wait, I suppose. Then she might go back to the camp. But she doesn't know the way very well, and she might get lost. Oh dear – I don't know which would be worse for Anne, being lost on the moor or a prisoner down here with us!'

'Perhaps she's neither,' said Jock, giving Timmy his last bit of sandwich. 'I must say I'm jolly glad to have Timmy. Honest, George, I couldn't believe it when I heard Tim whine, and then heard your voice, too. I thought I must be dreaming.'

They sat where they were for a little longer and then decided to go back to the tunnel where the train was. 'It's just possible we might find the switch that works the Open-Sesame bit,' said Julian. 'We ought to have looked before, really, but I didn't think of it.'

They went back to where the train stood silently on its pair of lines. It seemed such an ordinary old train now that the children couldn't imagine why they had ever thought it was strange and spooky.

They switched on the light again, then they looked about for any lever or handle that might perhaps open the hole in the wall. There didn't seem to be anything at all. They tried a few switches, but nothing happened.

Then George suddenly came across a big

lever low down in the brick wall itself. She tried to move it and couldn't. She called Julian.

'Ju! Come here. I wonder if this has got anything to do with opening that hole.'

The three boys came over to George. Julian tried to swing the lever down. Nothing happened. He pulled it but it wouldn't move. Then he and Dick pushed it upwards with all their strength.

And hey presto, there came a bang from somewhere, as something heavy shifted, and then a clanking as if machinery was at work. Then came the sliding, grating noise and a great piece of the brick wall moved slowly back, and then swung round sideways and stopped. The way of escape was open!

'Open Sesame!' said Dick, grandly, as the hole appeared.

'Better switch off the light here,' said Julian. 'If there's anyone still in the tunnel they might see the reflection of it on the tunnel-wall beyond, and wonder what it was.'

He stepped back and switched it off, and the

place was in darkness again. George put on her torch, and its feeble beam lighted up the way of escape.

'Come on,' said Dick, impatiently, and they all crowded out of the hole. 'We'll make for Olly's Yard.' They began to make their way down the dark tunnel.

'Listen,' said Julian, in a low voice. 'We'd better not talk at all, and we'd better go as quietly as we can. We don't know who may be in or out of this tunnel this evening. We don't want to walk bang into somebody.'

So they said nothing at all, but kept close to one another in single file, walking at the side of the track.

They had not gone more than a quarter of a mile before Julian stopped suddenly. The others bumped into one another, and Timmy gave a little whine as somebody trod on his paw. George's hand went down to his collar at once.

The four of them and Timmy listened, hardly daring to breathe. Somebody was coming up the tunnel towards them! They could see the pin-point of a torch, and hear the distant crunch of footsteps.

'Other way, quick!' whispered Julian, and they all turned. With Jock leading them now, they made their way as quickly and quietly as they could back to the place where the two tunnels met. They passed it and went on towards Kilty's Yard, hoping to get out that way.

But alas for their hopes, a lantern stood some way down the tunnel there, and they did not dare to go on. There might be nobody with the lantern – on the other hand there might. What were they to do?

'They'll see that hole in the wall is open!' suddenly said Dick. 'We left it open. They'll know we've escaped then. We're caught again! They'll come down to find us, and here we'll be!'

They stood still, pressed close together, Timmy growling a little in his throat. Then George remembered something!

'Julian! Dick! We could climb up that vent

that I came down,' she whispered. 'The one poor old Timmy fell down. Have we time?'

'Where is the vent?' said Julian, urgently. 'Quick, find it.'

George tried to remember. Yes, it was on the other side of the tunnel – near the place where the two tunnels met. She must look for the pile of soot. How she hoped the little light from her torch would not be seen. Whoever was coming up from Olly's Yard must be almost there by now!

She found the pile of soot that Timmy had fallen into. 'Here it is,' she whispered. 'But, oh Julian! How can we take Timmy?'

'We can't,' said Julian. 'We must hope he'll manage to hide and then slink out of the tunnel by himself. He's quite clever enough.'

He pushed George up the vent first and her feet found the first rungs. Then Jock went up, his nose almost on George's heels. Then Dick – and last of all, Julian. But before he managed to climb the first steps, something happened.

A bright glare filled the tunnel, as someone

switched on the light that hung there. Timmy slunk into the shadows and growled in his throat. Then there came a shout.

'Who's opened the hole in the wall? It's open! Who's there?'

It was Mr Andrews's voice. Then came another voice, angry and loud: 'Who's here? Who's opened this place?'

'Those kids can't have moved the lever,' said Mr Andrews. 'We bound them up tightly.'

The men, three of them, went quickly through the hole in the wall. Julian climbed up the first few rungs thankfully. Poor Timmy was left in the shadows at the bottom.

Out came the men at a run. 'They've gone! Their ropes are cut! How could they have escaped? We put Kit down one end of the tunnel and we've been walking up this end. Those kids must be about here somewhere.'

'Or hiding in the caves,' said another voice. 'Peters, go and look, while we hunt here.'

The men hunted everywhere. They had no idea that the vent was nearby in the wall. They did not see the dog that slunk by them like a shadow, keeping out of their way, and lying down whenever the light from a torch came near him.

George climbed steadily, feeling with her feet for the iron nails whenever she came to broken rungs. Then she came to a stop. Something was pressing on her head. What was it? She put up her hand to feel. It was the collection of broken iron bars that Timmy had fallen on that morning. He had dislodged some of them, and they had then fallen in such a way that they had lodged across the vent, all twined into each other. George could climb no higher. She tried to move the bars, but they were heavy and strong – besides, she was afraid she might bring the whole lot on top of her and the others. They might be badly injured then.

'What's up, George? Why don't you go on?' asked Jock, who was next.

'There's some iron bars across the vent – ones that must have fallen when Timmy fell,' said George. 'I can't go any higher! I daren't pull too hard at the bars.'

Jock passed the message to Dick, and he passed it down to Julian. The four of them came to a full-stop!

'Blow!' said Julian. 'I wish I'd gone up first. What are we to do now?'

What indeed? The four of them hung there in the darkness, hating the smell of the sooty old vent, miserably uncomfortable on the broken rungs and nails.

'How do you like adventures now, Jock?' asked Dick. 'I bet you wish you were in your own bed at home!'

'I don't!' said Jock. 'I wouldn't miss this for worlds! I always wanted an adventure – and I'm not grumbling at this one!'

[19]

What an adventure!

And now, what had happened to Anne? She had stumbled on and on for a long time, shouting to Mr Luffy. And outside his tent Mr Luffy sat, reading peacefully. But, as the evening came, and then darkness, he became very worried indeed about the five children.

He wondered what to do. It was hopeless for one man to search the moors. Half a dozen or more were needed for that! He decided to get his car and go over to Olly's Farm to get the men from there. So off he went.

But when he got there he found no one at home except Mrs Andrews and the little maid. Mrs Andrews looked bewildered and worried.

'What is the matter?' said Mr Luffy gently, as she came running out to the car, looking troubled.

'Oh, it's you, Mr Luffy,' she said, when he told her who he was. 'I didn't know who you were. Mr Luffy, something strange is happening. All the men have gone – and all the lorries, too. My husband has taken the car and nobody will tell me anything. I'm so worried.'

Mr Luffy decided not to add to her worries by telling her the children were missing. He just pretended he had come to collect some milk. 'Don't worry,' he said comfortingly to Mrs Andrews. 'You'll find things are all right in the morning, I expect. I'll come and see you then. Now I must be off on an urgent matter.'

He went bumping along the road in his car, puzzled. He had known there was something funny about Olly's Farm, and he had puzzled his brains a good deal over Olly's Yard and the spook-trains. He hoped the children hadn't got mixed up in anything dangerous.

'I'd better go down and report to the police that they're missing,' he thought. 'After all, I'm more or less responsible for them. It's very worrying indeed.'

He told what he knew at the police station, and the sergeant, an intelligent man, at once mustered six men and a police car.

'Have to find those kids,' he said. 'And we'll have to look into this Olly's Farm business, sir, and these here spook-trains, whatever they may be. We've known there was something funny going on, but we couldn't put our finger on it. But we'll find the children first.'

They went quickly up to the moors and the six men began to fan out to search, with Mr Luffy at the head. And the first thing they found was Anne!

She was still stumbling along, crying for Mr Luffy, but in a very small, weak voice now. When she heard his voice calling her in the darkness she wept for joy.

'Oh, Mr Luffy! You must save the boys,' she begged him. 'They're in that tunnel – and they've been caught by Mr Andrews and his men, I'm sure. They didn't come out and I waited and waited! Do come!'

'I've got some friends here who will certainly

come and help,' said Mr Luffy gently. He called the men, and in a few words told them what Anne had said.

'In the tunnel?' said one of them. 'Where the spook-trains run? Well, come on, men, we'll go down there.'

'You stay behind, Anne,' said Mr Luffy. But she wouldn't. So he carried her as he followed the men who were making their way through the heather, down to Olly's Yard. They did not bother with Wooden-Leg Sam. They went straight to the tunnel and walked up it quietly. Mr Luffy was a good way behind with Anne. She refused to stay with him in the yard.

'No,' she said, 'I'm not a coward. Really I'm not. I want to help to rescue the boys. I wish George was here. Where's George?'

Mr Luffy had no idea. Anne clung to his hand, scared but eager to prove that she was not a coward. Mr Luffy thought she was grand!

Meanwhile, Julian and the others had been in the vent for a good while, tired and uncomfortable. The men had searched in vain for them and were now looking closely into every niche at the sides of the tunnel.

And, of course, they found the vent! One of the men shone his light up it. It shone on to poor Julian's feet! The man gave a loud shout that almost made Julian fall off the rung he was standing on.

'Here they are! Up this vent. Who'd have thought it? Come on down or it'll be the worse for you!'

Julian didn't move. George pushed desperately at the iron bars above her head, but she could not move them. One of the men climbed up the vent and caught hold of Julian's foot.

He dragged so hard at it that the boy's foot was forced off the rung. Then the man dragged off the other foot, and Julian found himself hanging by his arms with the man tugging hard at his feet. He could hang on no longer. His tired arms gave way and he fell heavily down, landing half on the man and half on the pile of soot. Another man pounced on Julian at once, while the first climbed up the vent to find the next boy. Soon Dick felt his feet being tugged at, too.

'All right, all right. I'll come down!' he yelled, and climbed down. Then Jock climbed down, too. The men looked at them angrily.

'Giving us a chase like this! Who undid your ropes?' said Mr Andrews, roughly. One of the men put a hand on his arm and nodded up towards the vent. 'Someone else is coming down,' he said. 'We only tied up three boys, didn't we? Who's this, then?'

It was George, of course. She wasn't going to desert the three boys. Down she came, as black as night with soot.

'Another boy!' said the men. 'Where did he come from?'

'Any more up there?' asked Mr Andrews.

'Look and see,' said Julian, and got a box on the ears for his answer.

'Treat them rough now,' ordered Peters. 'Teach them a lesson, the little pests. Take them away.'

The children's hearts sank. The men caught hold of them roughly. Blow! Now they would be made prisoners again.

Suddenly a cry came from down the tunnel: 'Police! Run for it!'

The men dropped the children's arms at once and stood undecided. A man came tearing up the tunnel. 'I tell you the police are coming!' he gasped. 'Are you stone deaf? There's a whole crowd of them. Run for it! Somebody's split on us.'

'Get along to Kilty's Yard!' shouted Peters. 'We can get cars there. Run for it!'

To the children's dismay, the men tore down the tunnel to Kilty's Yard. They would escape! They heard the sound of the men's feet as they ran along the line.

George found her voice. 'Timmy! Where are you? After them, Timmy! Stop them!'

A black shadow came streaking by out of the hole in the wall, where Timmy had been hiding and watching for a chance to come to George. He had heard her voice and obeyed. He raced after the men like a greyhound, his tongue hanging out, panting as he went.

These were the men who had ill-treated George and the others, were they? Aha, Timmy knew how to deal with people like that!

The policemen came running up, and Mr Luffy and Anne came up behind them.

'They've gone down there, with Timmy after them,' shouted George. The men looked at her and gasped. She was black all over. The others were filthy dirty too, with sooty-black faces in the light of the lamp that still shone down from the wall of the tunnel.

'George!' shrieked Anne in delight. 'Julian! Oh, are you all safe? I went back to tell Mr Luffy about you and I got lost. I'm so ashamed!'

'You've nothing to be ashamed of, Anne,' said Mr Luffy. 'You're a grand girl! Brave as a lion!'

From down the tunnel came shouts and yells and loud barks. Timmy was at work! He had caught up with the men and launched himself on them one after another, bringing each one heavily to the ground. They were terrified to find a big animal growling and snapping all around them. Timmy held them at bay in the tunnel, not allowing them to go one step further, snapping at any man who dared to go near.

The police ran up. Timmy growled extra fiercely just to let the men know that it was quite impossible to get by him. In a trice each of the men was imprisoned by a pair of strong arms and they were being told to come quietly.

They didn't go quietly. For one thing Mr Andrews lost his nerve and howled dismally. Jock felt very ashamed of him.

'Shut up,' said a burly policeman. 'We know you're only the miserable little cat's-paw – taking money from the big men to hold your tongue and obey orders.'

Timmy barked as if to say, 'Yes, don't you dare call him a *dog's* paw! That would be too good a name for him!'

'Well, I don't think I ever in my life saw

dirtier children,' said Mr Luffy. 'I vote we all go back to my car and I drive the lot of you over to Olly's Farm for a meal and a bath!'

So back they all went, tired, dirty, and also feeling very thrilled.

What a night! They told Anne all that had happened, and she told them her story, too. She almost fell asleep in the car as she talked, she was so tired.

Mrs Andrews was sensible and kind, though upset to hear that her husband had been taken off by the police. She got hot water for baths, and laid a meal for the hungry children.

'I wouldn't worry overmuch, Mrs Andrews,' said kindly Mr Luffy. 'That husband of yours needs a lesson, you know. This will probably keep him going straight in future. The farm is yours, and you can now hire proper farm-workers who will do what you want them to do. And I think Jock will be happier without a stepfather for the present.'

'You're right, Mr Luffy,' said Mrs Andrews, wiping her eyes quickly. 'Quite right. I'll let

Jock help me with the farm, and get it going beautifully. To think that Mr Andrews was in with all those black marketeers! It's that friend of his, you know, who makes him do all this. He's so weak. He knew Jock was snooping about in that tunnel, and that's why he wanted him to go away – and kept making him have a boy here or go out with him. I knew there was something funny going on.'

'No wonder he was worried when Jock took it into his head to go and camp with our little lot,' said Mr Luffy.

'To think of that old yard and tunnel being used again!' said Mrs Andrews. 'And all those tales about spook-trains – and the way they hid that train, and hid all the stuff, too. Why, it's like a fairy tale, isn't it!'

She ran to see if the water was hot for the baths. It was, and she went to call the children, who were in the big bedroom next door. She opened it and looked in. Then she called Mr Luffy upstairs.

He looked in at the door, too. The five, and

Timmy, were lying on the floor in a heap, waiting for the bathwater. They hadn't liked to sit on chairs or beds, they were so dirty. And they had fallen asleep where they sat, their faces as black as a sweep's.

'Talk about black marketeers!' whispered Mrs Andrews. 'Anyone would think we'd got the whole lot of them here in the bedroom!'

They all woke up and went to have a bath one by one, and a good meal after that. Then back to camp with Mr Luffy, Jock with them, too.

It was glorious to snuggle down into the sleeping-bags. George called out to the three boys.

'Now don't you dare to go off without me tonight, see?'

'The adventure is over,' called back Dick. 'How did you like it, Jock?'

'Like it?' said Jock, with a happy sigh. 'It was simply – smashing!'